th **MAGI**
SAMAR **IND**

Alan Temperley was born and grew up in Sunderland. As a boy he kept mice, sang in a big church choir, played cricket and rugby, enjoyed stories and knocked around on his bike. At the age of sixteen he joined the Merchant Navy. Later he became a teacher of English in the Scottish Highlands. Now he is an award-winning author whose work has been widely translated and televised. His two wishes are that you live life to the full and that you will be kind to all animals.

'I defy anyone, boy or girl, not to be caught up in the magic of this robust, thrilling adventure'   *Scotsman*

'Packed with beautifully narrated action'   *Guardian*

'Temperley's world is one of wicked wizards, treasures, golden domes and spells . . . good books work their own magic when character, plot and fine writing combine to take us places'   *Irish Times*

'An exciting moral tale of how courage and goodness triumph over power and greed'   *TES*

'Temperley writes with terrific style'   *Sunday Herald*

For Lauren,
with love

the MAGICIAN of SAMARKAND

ALAN TEMPERLEY

Illustrated by ADAM STOWER

MACMILLAN CHILDREN'S BOOKS

First published 2003 by Macmillan Children's Books Ltd

This edition published 2004 by Macmillan Children's Books
a division of Macmillan Publishers Limited
20 New Wharf Road, London NI 9RR
Basingstoke and Oxford
www.panmacmillan.com

Associated companies throughout the world

ISBN 0 330 41573 5

5 7 9 8 6 4

A CIP catalogue record for this book is available from the British Library.

Phototypeset by Intype Libra Ltd
Printed and bound in Great Britain by Mackays of Chatham plc, Kent

Contents

Zohak Ali

Zohak Ali came out of the desert. It was dawn. Behind him a train of one hundred camels and fifty elephants, each heavily laden with treasure and led by a barefoot slave, plodded through the sand. Before him the minarets and golden domes of Samarkand were lit by the rising sun.

The guard at the western gate saw him far off and as soon as the hour of prayer was past a small crowd gathered on the city wall.

Among them stood Anahita, daughter of Kashgar, the shoemaker. She wore a blue shawl for the morning was cool. With wide eyes she watched the caravan draw near.

Zohak Ali was a magnificent figure. Robes of dark silk billowed about him and he rode a beautiful white camel. Beneath a black turban shot with scarlet, his eyes were fierce as an eagle's. His nose was hooked, his jutting beard challenged the world. Three tigers at his right side and three panthers at his left tugged their long leashes.

The city gates opened to admit him but Zohak Ali reined his camel to a halt. Adjusting the jewelled dagger thrust through his sash, he glanced up at the merchants and traders above him. Among them, beautiful as a pearl among shells, stood a girl. His eyes flashed. Then Zohak Ali turned to face the mile-long train that followed in his wake.

To one side of the great western gate they made camp. Anahita leaned over the parapet, marvelling as the laden camels and elephants arrived beneath her: nets filled with golden ornaments; cages of rare birds and animals; oriental tapestries; baskets of precious stones; statues carved from jade and ivory; sandalwood chests; myriad-coloured silk; big stone jars of oil and perfume.

All these Anahita recognized. She had seen similar treasures in the palace of Sultan Mushtaq. But what was that big red book, chained and padlocked, that swung from his saddle? What were the globes and symbols and astrolabes and open crates of strange apparatus? She asked a man of learning who stood nearby. He did not know.

A great tent was erected for Zohak Ali. It was the tent of a sheikh, white and gold and scarlet. Flags flew above. Rugs and chests were carried within.

* *.* .* * . .* * *. 2 * *.* .: * . *.

On all sides, spreading across the desert like a second town, the army of slaves set up tents for themselves. Their backs were naked, they wore bright pantaloons tied at the ankle. Cooking fires sent trails of smoke into the morning air.

Zohak Ali withdrew into his tent where his body slaves had prepared sherbet and sweetmeats. But before he did so he shaded his eyes and looked up at the crowd on the wall.

The girl in the blue shawl had gone.

Anahita lived with her father, mother and older brother in a little house in a busy alley behind the market. They were a poor family. Her father, Kashgar al Kharif, was a good man, the best maker of shoes and saddles for a hundred miles around, as truly an artist as the builders of the Great Mosque in the market square. But such painstaking work took a long time. He earned little money.

Anahita's mother, Fatima, had been very beautiful, and still was, though since the birth of her children she had grown rather fat. Her fondness for pastries may have had something to do with this. Fatima was a merry wife and mother but sometimes she got cross with her husband because he was not a better businessman.

Anahita's brother, Farraj, was fifteen years old and handsome. Often she saw her friends peeping at him. He worked with his father who privately declared that in time Farraj would become the finest saddle-maker in the whole of Asia.

On the morning of Zohak Ali's arrival, Anahita hurried home to tell them about the great caravan.

Fatima clapped her hands. 'Oh, how wonderful! What news! A rich stranger. And he looked at you, you say? Tell us again.'

But Anahita's father said: 'Be quiet. What are you talking about?' He frowned. 'I don't like it. Who is this man? Where has he come from? How can any honest person be as rich as the Sultan? And what are these strange charts and instruments you tell us about? There will be trouble, you mark my words.'

'I will go this evening.' Farraj wore his work apron. 'See what I can find out.'

'Quite right, work comes first. You are a good boy.' Kashgar rumpled his son's black hair and looked from the window. Already the shadows had retreated halfway down the houses opposite. 'Come along, Anahita. We can't stand talking all day. I have shoes to make. You have a saddle to deliver to Prince Sohrab.'

She did not need reminding. Anahita loved visiting the Sultan's palace. It was cool there, with gardens and running water. The Sultan, Mushtaq the Magnificent, was a kind and generous ruler. His son, Sohrab, Prince of the Golden Turban, was loved throughout the city.

Carrying the heavy saddle, Anahita made her way through the thronging market and climbed the streets to the palace. Greenery tumbled down the mosaic walls. The gates were open. At each side stood a tremendous guard with a scimitar. Anahita told one her business. He escorted her across the courtyard and through an arch to lawns where peacocks wandered and deer grazed beneath fruit trees.

Beyond lay the Sultan's riding arena. In stables at one side lived the racing camels, at the other his Arab racehorses. Normally Anahita delivered a saddle to one of the servants. This day, however, as she drew close she saw that the Sultan and his son were at that moment looking over their mounts. A groom led a beautiful stallion from its stall. She drew back but the Sultan saw her and beckoned her forward. Nervously Anahita approached. She had never spoken to the Sultan or his son before and salaamed deeply.

'Come, my child,' said Sultan Mushtaq. 'You must be the daughter of our most excellent Kashgar.' He lifted her chin. 'And how beautiful you are growing! Is she not, Sohrab?'

Anahita blushed easily. Conscious of her poor clothes and humble position, she glanced up. The Sultan was smiling.

'Hush, Father. You embarrass her.' Prince Sohrab took the saddle and examined the workmanship. 'Did you ever see such leather and stitching? In truth, Kashgar al Kharif is a treasure to our city. Tell him,'

he said to Anahita, 'that I shall use it in the races tomorrow. And ask him, if he will, to come to the palace the day after. I need new saddles for my racing camels and a pair of riding boots.'

'Thank you, your highness.' Anahita lowered her eyes. 'I will tell him.'

'Now go to the kitchen, child,' Mushtaq said kindly. 'You must be hot after the steep streets. They will give you a cooling drink. And here,' he plucked a ripe pomegranate, 'they are sweet.'

Anahita took it. 'Thank you, Excellency.' Touching her brow and bowing again, she retreated.

The guard, who had been standing a few paces apart, escorted Anahita through arches and watered gardens to the palace kitchens.

Prince Sohrab watched her go. 'You are right, Father,' he said. 'She is very pretty.'

The Blue Palace

Zohak Ali reclined on cushions. The air was perfumed. A servant approached, bearing a platter. On it lay roast hummingbirds, hares' tongues, Muscat grapes, goldfinch breasts and other delicacies. Zohak fed a morsel to his favourite falcon and waved the man away.

A slave fanned cooling air. Through a slit in the door curtain the great magician glimpsed the wall of Samarkand. At last he had arrived. In this most beautiful of cities he would build his palace, a palace greater than that of the Sultan himself. It had been a long journey, a quest that had led him to and fro across Asia and north Africa for twenty years. Who, seeing him in his present splendour, could guess his history? He sipped sweet wine and remembered:

He had been born in Egypt, the son of a Nile boatman and a fat obeah woman from the Congo. Zohak had been her favourite, listening to her tales of voodoo, sleeping at her side in the rocking cabin. His father and the rest of the family were excluded. She taught him her black magic, spreading sticks and bones and chicken blood on the deck. The little boy clapped his hands as she described how people who crossed her were struck by misfortune. She was the centre of his world. Until that terrible day when she was denounced as a witch and burned to death in the street. Zohak blamed his father and the girl from Cairo he married two days later. He hated them and he hated his brothers and sisters who sat on their stepmother's lap and showered her with hugs and kisses. He wanted revenge. And so, one night when everyone was asleep, he stole his father's savings, locked them all in the cabin and set fire to the barge. Waiting only long enough to enjoy the spectacle and ensure the boat sank, he fled to Baghdad. He was ten years old.

The money was soon gone. Seeing the handsome Egyptian boy in the slave market, the Caliph of Baghdad had bought him as a house servant and dressed him in white livery, the colour of angels and innocence. For seven years he served the Caliph and became a favourite of the household, though not of the other servants to whom his manner was arrogant. By simple magic he gained advantage. By judicious theft, laying blame at the hands of slaves less trusted — several of whom had those hands or their heads chopped off — he became rich enough to buy his freedom.

For seven more years, in the libraries, dens and covens of Baghdad and in his smoke-filled laboratory, he studied sorcery and the magician's arts. Day by day his knowledge grew until, by the end of this time, he was one of the richest and most powerful men in the city. He was also, through treachery and suspected murder, one of the most hated – so hated that one dawn, after a night of rioting, crowds had stoned him from the gates.

From Baghdad, burdened by nothing but his leather-bound book of spells, the distillation of all those years of learning, he had travelled to far Peking. Having become rich once, Zohak reasoned, he could become rich again. Within a day of his arrival it reached his ears that the young Emperor of China in his Summer Palace was headstrong and foolish. A month later the newcomer was introduced and dazzled the court with a colourful display of magic. The emperor applauded; he wanted more of the amusing magician; he demanded that he must live in the palace like a jester. But the jesting did not last long. Before the emperor was twenty-one, Zohak Ali had become the possessor of half the imperial fortune. It was not difficult: gambling, sorcery, a little midnight theft, intercepting the camel trains. But the pampered and all-powerful emperor did not like it. Nor did his advisers. Zohak Ali was thrown into the dragon pit.

There followed a battle, one of the greatest spectacles ever seen in Peking, in which the dragon was slain and the magician so badly wounded it seemed impossible he would live. The cheering crowds departed. Somehow Zohak Ali dragged himself out from beneath the dragon's coils. Everything was lost – or almost everything. As he slipped away by night, hidden beneath straw and dung in an ox-cart, two items went with him. One was his big red book of spells – the longer he studied, the thicker it grew. The second, secreted beneath his clothes, was a fabulous gem, the star of the imperial crown. It was known as the Bangalore diamond, big as an egg, the most famous jewel in the world.

It took him many years to recover but recover he did and in the end no burn remained, no limp, no scar but a slash on one cheek which he left because it added to his dashing appearance.

During this time he resumed his studies and travelled widely. And it was back in Egypt, a long time later, that a divining rod in the shape of a scorpion revealed to him the location of the ancient tombs of the Pharaohs. An army of slaves wielding pickaxes and shovels descended upon the Valley of the Kings and carried off the gold and jewelled treasure to his fort in the desert. The Pharaohs' mummified remains were flung on to bonfires. Rumour of this reached the king in Cairo who was, understandably, more than a little cross at the disrespect being shown to his ancestors. Moreover, he wanted the riches himself to wage war against his Syrian neighbours. Thus, in a surprise raid one morning, Zohak Ali found himself seized, accused, pronounced guilty, bound, drenched in goat's blood and flung into the crocodile-infested waters of the Nile.

From the stones of Baghdad, the dragon of China and the crocodiles of Egypt he had narrowly escaped with his life. Now he came to the golden city of Samarkand between the mountains and the desert. Here, at the crossroads of the continent, his ambition to become the richest, most powerful and most feared man in the whole of Asia would finally be accomplished.

But they had been travelling all night and now he was weary. Zohak Ali clapped his hands for music. A slave girl began to dance. Ringed by his big purring cats, the magician closed his eyes and slept.

Work on the Blue Palace began that very day and lasted for a year. Architects had been sent ahead to buy land, high land from where it was possible to look down into the alleys and courtyards of the city and across it to the palace of Sultan Mushtaq. Some owners had been reluctant to sell. Visitors in the night persuaded them.

A thousand workmen demolished the buildings on the hilltop site. From east, west, north and south, wagons and caravans descended upon Samarkand. The foundations were laid. Walls sprang up. Zohak Ali whipped his builders to exhaustion. A thousand were not enough and one morning they awoke to discover that all had acquired twin brothers overnight. They looked identical and had the same memories. Which was the original workman, which the twin? Soon they became triplets. Three thousand builders sweated on the site from dawn till dusk.

The city was amazed at the rate the palace grew. For only creatures of the night knew that while good people slept, Zohak Ali roamed from room to room working his magic: adding a metre to the walls here, completing an arch there, sinking a well to provide sweet water.

In precisely 365 days it was complete, a blue-green palace quite unlike the white palace of Sultan Mushtaq and, as the Nile boatman's son intended, even more magnificent. It was well protected, on one side by a cliff, on three by lions and cheetahs, tigers and leopards which roamed the perimeter gardens. Fountains played in the courtyards; mosaic covered the floors; a breathtaking tower, higher than the Great Mosque in the market square, soared above the city. His banner, a black phoenix ringed by seven red stars on a yellow ground, flew from the roof. And deep within the hills beneath the palace, a labyrinth of caves and vaulted cellars provided storage for Zohak Ali's treasure. Its existence was a secret, for as soon as the work was completed he gave the labourers a cordial to drink. It was a mixture of fruit juice, nepenthe leaves and water of Lethe. As soon as they had drunk it, the labyrinth was wiped from their memories.

The baggage camels and elephants were despatched

back to the desert. The builders, no longer triplets, were paid off. Attended by one hundred slaves and servants, Zohak Ali settled into his new abode.

Right from the start it was known as the Blue Palace.

Every morning, after rounds of the palace and an hour or two in his study, the magician opened a hidden door and descended into the labyrinth. Lamp in hand, he gloated over his mounds of gold and blazing gems, fabulous ornaments and the grinning skulls of adversaries.

Afterwards he climbed a flight of spiral stairs to the top of the tower. They ended in a dark chamber where an arrangement of mirrors and lenses reflected an image of the moving city on to a white table. It was a camera obscura. Standing in the darkness, he watched Samarkand pass before him, followed individuals with a crooked finger, raked the city towards him like spilled coffee beans as if he would possess it all. He loved the secrecy, the sense of power it gave him to see and be unseen. Sometimes, if there were people he wished to spy on, he would remain there half the day.

A door led to the high balcony. Having adjusted his turban, Zohak Ali stepped out into the blinding sunlight to be seen by the whole city. Black robes billowing, he stared from the Sultan's palace to the rooftops and sprawling streets that lay below.

Sometimes, hands braced on the parapet, he spotted

the girl he had seen on the city wall. Hook-nosed and high up as an eagle, he watched Anahita hurry along alleys and through the crowded market. He saw how, for a few small coins, she bought cheap meat and rice and over-ripe fruit for her mother. He discovered where she lived. And more than once, hiding his fine clothes beneath a cloak, he followed her through the streets. She was even more beautiful than he remembered, the most beautiful girl he had ever seen.

In his lonely palace, as the molten sun sank into the desert, she troubled his thoughts. Love was something Zohak Ali did not understand. Hatred and passion, yes. Love, no. But as he looked out on the darkening velvet night, he longed to possess Anahita as he possessed so many desirable objects. For a man in his position, it was true, her lowly birth was regrettable. Still, once he had paid her father and dispatched the family to some distant location, once he had dressed her in fine clothes and jewels, who would remember? She would be among the most exquisite of his ornaments, more lovely, certainly, than any of the wives of Sultan Mushtaq. Strolling in his rose garden or serving coffee in his blue-green palace, she would bring him honour. Perhaps, he smiled at the thought, he would even make her his wife, at least for as long as she was young and pleased him. Afterwards, when her beauty was gone and he grew tired of her . . .

Laughter and a chatter of young voices rose from the streets below. Closer at hand one of his tigers roared.

Perhaps it had made a kill — some night intruder. It was what he deserved.

The great magician turned from his star-spangled window. The room was spacious and magnificent. It was also, apart from a caged linnet, deserted. He struck a gong.

For ten seconds no one appeared.

He struck it again — hard. And again. *Bong! Bong! Bong! Bong!*

A flustered slave ran through the doorway.

'Must I beat the gong all night?' Zohak Ali belaboured him with the hammer.

The slave covered his head. 'I am sorry, Master. Only for one second I—'

'Keep me waiting again and I will have you flogged!'

'Yes, Master.' He bowed in submission.

In the wake of that distant laughter the silence was suffocating.

'Song!' Zohak Ali gathered his robes about him. 'And dancing — that new girl from Kashmir.' He fell to a couch draped in silk and covered with cushions. 'Bring me my hookah.'

The slave ran off.

The magician closed his heavy-lidded eyes and made plans for Anahita. How much, he wondered, would her father expect? What should he offer?

A Proposal

Anahita had not seen the cloaked magician shadowing her through the streets; had no more reason than the shabbiest beggar in the market to think Zohak Ali was taking an interest in her. Why should he – he was older than her father. The remote, billowing figure the whole city saw from time to time on his tower meant no more to Anahita than he did to Farraj and his friends. In fact less, for her thoughts were elsewhere. Twice Prince Sohrab had reined his horse in the street and once called his bearers to halt in order to speak to her. His black eyes sparkled, his smile was kind, her father's reins were looped in his strong hands. Anahita was half in love, and every evening as she sat in the lamplight her daydreams were full of the young prince.

Sohrab, meanwhile, not much more than a boy with the first moustache darkening his lip, was like any other young man. He enjoyed talking to an innocent and lovely girl. Though their situations were impossibly different, when he rode into town he looked for the daughter of his saddle-maker. He ordered shoes he did not need so that she might bring them to the palace. In quiet moments he recalled the shy look in her eyes and the blush that rose to her cheeks each time they met.

Little escaped the gaze of Zohak Ali. He had seen the young prince lean from his saddle to speak to Anahita. Though love was unknown to him, that did not mean he was blind to it in fools. It gave his plan to take Anahita to the Blue Palace an added sweetness. For he hated Sultan Mushtaq and his family. He hated their riches — even though he planned to acquire these for himself. He hated the way they were respected throughout the city. He believed the Sultan should have invited a man as important as himself to a feast, or at least to dine. But the Sultan had not and Zohak's own invitation had been politely declined. So to snatch Anahita from before the eyes of the prince would be a small but satisfying revenge. A start.

And so, late one morning, Zohak Ali descended the precipitous streets below the Blue Palace and made his way through the crowded market. His cloaks blew, taking the space of five; the Bangalore diamond glittered in his black turban; a peacock plume flew above. Traders shrank aside. Dogs cowered, snarling.

Like Moses crossing the Red Sea, the way opened before him.

A honking goose ran into his path. Zohak Ali scowled and rapped it with his staff. There was an explosion of feathers. As if it had been kicked by a stallion, the goose flew sideways and hit its owner in the face. The bird was dead.

'Hey!' The stall-holder dabbed blood from his nose. He was angry. 'You can buy that. That goose cost money.' He thrust it into the magician's face.

'Out of my way.' Zohak Ali tried to brush him aside.

But the stall-holder was a sturdy man. He pushed back. 'I know you own that great palace up there. But that don't give you the right to start trampling over us poor traders trying to make an honest living.'

'That's right.' Others backed him up. 'You're not short of a shekel or two. Pay him for the goose.'

He was surrounded. But Zohak Ali did not lack courage. He laid about him with the staff. And as he did so, terrible things happened: a threatening fist turned white with leprosy; stinging flies, thick as a rug, descended upon the stall-holder; maggots swarmed over his meat; a nearby vegetable stall collapsed beneath the weight of locusts; a mad dog, foaming at the mouth, ran through the market.

The crowd fell back. Zohak Ali looked about him, eyes burning. Without a word he went on his way. No one dared to call out. No one flung a rock.

He entered the maze of alleyways that lay beyond

the market. Lines of washing criss-crossed overhead. Old ladies sat on chairs. Dogs scratched. Little shops and rickety stalls stood on either side. Soon he came to the workshop of Kashgar al Kharif. It faced the narrow street. The house stood behind. Ducking his head, Zohak Ali entered the shadows and found the shoe-maker and his son working at benches.

When Kashgar saw his visitor he was startled. Quickly he spat a mouthful of tacks into his hand and salaamed respectfully.

Zohak Ali ignored the greeting and stared from young Farraj to the crowded shelves around.

'What brings Zohak Ali to the workshop of a man as poor as myself?' Kashgar said at length. 'Is your honour seeking shoes?'

'Shoes? No.' The magician turned. 'You have a daughter, I believe.'

'I do, sir,' replied Kashgar. 'And a son. My wife and children are the lights of my life.'

'I care nothing for the others,' said Zohak Ali. 'It is your daughter in whom my interest lies.'

'Anahita?' said Kashgar. 'Why? Has she displeased your honour in some way?'

'Displeased?' Zohak Ali permitted himself a thin smile. 'No, pleased, rather. I wish to marry her.'

'To marry her?' Kashgar was astonished, horrified. 'Perhaps your honour has made some mistake.'

'No mistake. I do not make mistakes.'

'But she is only a girl, not old enough yet to take a husband. I am sure—'

'On the day of the wedding,' Zohak ignored his protests, 'I shall give you five hundred gold coins. You will be rich.'

'Rich! You think I will sell my daughter like a slave girl?'

'Why not? When you have had time to consider, I am sure you will find it a good bargain.'

'A good bargain? You think I will bargain? For the happiness of Anahita?'

'Of course. What other use is a daughter? And why should she not be happy? Mistress of my most beautiful palace; the wealthiest woman in Samarkand. Naturally she will be happy.' Zohak Ali threw an end of his robe over his shoulder. 'The wedding will take place three weeks from today. The date is auspicious. The new moon will be in—'

The inner door burst open and Anahita came running into the workshop. 'Mother is asking—' She saw Zohak Ali. Her hand flew to her mouth. 'Oh, I didn't know—'

'Of course not, child,' said Kashgar. 'Now, come here.' He drew her forward. 'It is well you should listen. This gentleman has a proposition he wishes to put to you.'

'To me?' Anahita retreated behind her father's shoulder. 'A proposition?' Her eyes were frightened.

'Not to her,' said Zohak. 'She is merely a girl, this is no concern of hers. I speak to her father.'

'No,' said Kashgar. 'We must hear what Anahita has to say.'

Farraj crossed to his sister's side. 'You are safe.' He put a protective arm around her. 'No one is going to hurt you.'

'Yes, daughter, a proposition,' said Kashgar. 'You know who this is?'

She nodded.

'He is master of the Blue Palace.'

'I know.'

'He is very rich.'

'Yes.' It was a whisper.

'Listen carefully,' her father said. 'He wishes to marry you.'

'To marry . . . me?' Anahita stared at Zohak Ali. With a clear gaze she saw his lined forehead and hollow cheeks, the cruel eyes, his long wrinkled fingers bedecked with rings. All so different from the young Prince Sohrab.

'No!' she exclaimed. 'Oh, Father, no! You can't wish me to— Oh, I can't! Not a man as old as . . . Oh!'

She pulled from her brother's arm and ran out of the workshop. Her cries reached them from within the house.

'Sir.' Kashgar tried to lessen the insult. 'You do my humble family a great honour. But you see how it is. She is young and—'

Zohak Ali was furious. That he, the richest man for a thousand miles around, destined to become the greatest ruler in Asia, should be rejected by the daughter of a shoemaker!

'I shall not forget this, Kashgar al Kharif.' He struck out with his staff. A bundle of shoes, a block of beeswax, a bale of leather burst into flame. Yellow fire ran along the shelves. 'If you are wise you will not cross my path again.'

He swept from the shop.

Kashgar and Farraj beat at the fire with brooms, muffled it with a rug, flung jugs of water. The flames were extinguished.

Fatima ran through from the house. 'You brute!' she cried. 'What have you been saying to—' She halted and took in the smoking ruin of the shop.

'He has gone,' said Kashgar.

'I will kill him!' Farraj blazed with anger.

'No.' Kashgar restrained his impetuous son. 'Zohak Ali is a dangerous man. We must be careful.'

'Marry Anahita!' exclaimed Fatima who longed for a rich husband for her daughter. 'A man who would do this! I would rather she married the poorest camel driver in the whole of Samarkand.'

Stoned from
the City

Zohak Ali slammed his study door, threw over
a chair, flung a flask of smoking liquid at the wall.
He had never been more angry. Beyond his window lay
the garden, almost a jungle already. A leopard clawed
the trunk of a palm tree — it would soon be feeding
time. The magician pulled open a drawer. Within lay
a scatter of children's toys, a little wooden menagerie.
He took out a prettily-carved goat and tossed it from
the window. For a few seconds it lay in the grass then
suddenly became a real goat. The leopard spotted it.
The goat raced away, bleating wildly, but the leopard
was too fast. In five bounds it pulled the goat down and
clamped its jaws on the unfortunate creature's neck.
Zohak Ali watched as the leopard began to feed.

His study, the hub of the palace and all his power,

was a large, bright room. Sunlight streamed through a second set of windows which looked out over the city. The fireplace, for the winters were cold, was covered by a screen of iridescent hummingbirds. Half of one wall was devoted to his library, rare books of alchemy, sorcery and the rest which he had collected on his travels. Beside these stood a single easy chair and a table upon which were set a freshly-filled lamp and his smoking apparatus. In this part of the study, beautiful rugs from Ankara and Tashkent were spread on a polished wooden floor.

The opposite side of the study was different, more like a laboratory. Here the floor was mosaic tiles. Shelves from knee-height to the ceiling were stacked with jars and phials, powders, liquids, roots, bones, insects, all the ingredients required for his spells. Not that all the spells needed ingredients: for many, words were enough; for others, gestures; some needed all three. On a number of tables in that part of the room, experiments were in progress.

In the middle of the study, library on one side, laboratory on the other, stood the magician's desk. On it, the quintessence of his power, lay his big, leather-bound book of spells. It was the fruit of his lifetime of study. Whatever magic he wanted, from plagues to whirlwinds to giving people the heads of birds, could be found between its faded red covers. Most of the spells he knew by heart, certainly those he used at all frequently, but they had to be *exact*. For this reason they had to be written down. Zohak Ali still remembered the day when, attempting to quieten a very expensive new camel, he had concluded a simple spell with the syllables *nye-see-ink* instead of the correct *nye-she-ann*. As a result the unfortunate animal, instead of becoming calm, had burst into flame. The event had taken place in a camel market and caused a considerable stir.

In order to protect the volume, he had ringed his desk with alarms, magical hoops that it was impossible to cross without filling the palace with a clangour of bells. Household slaves had been warned never to approach within a metre and taken to the snake-filled punishment pit in the garden to see what would happen to anyone who did. Finally, Zohak Ali never purchased a slave who could read, and ensured by a potent spell that none would ever be able to do so.

Leaving the leopard with its half-devoured prey, he walked the study, looked down on the city, retreated to his desk. Before him lay the book of spells. Normally, if his spirits were low, a flick through the yellowed, handwritten pages cheered him up, even made him laugh, but not today. He pushed it aside so violently that it fell to the floor. She had rejected him, called him old! A shoemaker's daughter! Surrounded by his potions and experiments, Zohak Ali brooded over what had occurred.

The following days brought little relief. He longed for revenge. Death was too simple. The big red book offered many alternatives. He made his choice. From the top of the tower he saw Anahita in the street but she was too far off for his magic to work. He hurried down but by the time he arrived she was gone.

On other forays into the city he sipped coffee and gazed contemptuously on the passers-by. What were the common herd to him? On the very day of his arrival he had sent spies out into the courtyards, alleyways and rich houses of the town. Now in dark chambers he met them and listened to their reports. Slowly his plans to rob the citizens of their savings, to milk them dry and bring the whole of Samarkand under his control, were taking shape.

The people, meanwhile, were troubled by a different problem — or two problems. Several scores of men, women and children had gone missing. Wives had lost husbands, sons hunted for their mothers, fathers wept for their missing daughters.

At the same time there was a sudden rise in the number of stray dogs, donkeys and other creatures wandering the city. No matter that they were starving, they were a public nuisance. They pestered grieving families, dirtied the streets, stole meat and vegetables from the stalls of traders and started a plague of fleas. Where were they all coming from? Wherever it was, people declared angrily, it could not be allowed to continue. They were a danger to health, they should be put down, exterminated.

It was Anahita, on the very day that *she* went missing, who first discovered what was happening.

It was a blazing hot afternoon. Most people had stopped work and withdrawn into the shade or their cool white houses until the streets became more bearable. Kashgar, however, following the damage to his shop, could not afford to lay down his tools and Anahita had been dispatched to deliver a pair of fine red shoes to a customer at the edge of the city.

As she hurried along, her head covered to protect it from the sun, the only other person in the shimmering street was a lame pedlar, a ragged boy of eight or ten with a cart upon which lay a handful of withered vegetables. Anahita was catching him up when without warning another figure appeared from a side-alley. It was Zohak Ali. He walked swiftly, his mind on other matters. Headlong he collided with the handcart. A wheel came off. The magician stumbled. Furious, he turned his gaze upon the frightened pedlar boy. He raised his staff, a staff with a head like a venomous snake. Anahita froze, expecting to see the boy receive a beating. But the second the staff struck him the pedlar disappeared. In his place stood a starving and bedraggled kitten. It too was lame. The magician lashed out at it. The kitten sprang aside. He strode after it and struck again, a blow that would have broken its back. The kitten ran the other way. With a scowl he left it cowering beneath the toppled cart and turned up the street.

Anahita dodged into a camel yard. She was too late, the magician had seen her and recognized her. Swiftly he followed.

The camels rested beneath dirty awnings. Their jaws munched sideways. Sleepily they regarded the people who had come among them.

Anahita could find no way of escape. She crouched behind a mother and calf. They only half hid her.

Zohak Ali stood several paces distant. 'Such a queen I could have made you,' he said. 'That face, those eyes, the way you hold your head. Instead,' his lips writhed, 'how I hate you!'

'Sir,' Anahita rose. She was so frightened she could hardly speak. 'I am truly sorry if I have—'

'Sorry? What do I care for your sorrow? You are nothing. An arrangement of features that men call beautiful. But I tell you this: Prince Sohrab,' he spat to cleanse his mouth, 'will never rein his horse to speak to you again. No man will see your face without turning his eyes away. I warned you, did I not? I warned you all.'

It was the moment he had been waiting for. The spell was on his lips. The great magician tossed back his cape and pointed at her with his staff:

'Youth and beauty
Turn to dust,
Crooked, forgotten
And accursed:
Pik! Raka! Shah!'

Anahita staggered as what felt like a torrent of ice-cold air hit her in the chest. It ran up into her face and down through her body, a shrinking, crinkly, stiffening sensation. She cried aloud and covered her face with her hands. The feeling stopped. Anahita raised her head, or tried to, but her back would not straighten. The hands before her eyes were those of an old woman, wrinkled and crooked as claws. The sinews of her wrists stood out like string. Coarse grey hair straggled across her eyes.

Zohak Ali laughed. 'There, go on your way. Withered old hag! See how many men's heads you turn today.'

Merrier than he had been for a long time, he pulled the gates wide and was gone into the deserted street.

Anahita was terrified. She examined her shrivelled arms, hitched up her skirt to see her stick-like legs. A drinking trough for the camels stood at the end of the yard. Dreading what she would discover, she drew back the hanks of hair and bowed above it. An ancient woman with puckered lips, a sprinkling of warts and pock-marked cheeks gazed back from the still water. It was a face so different from the one she knew that Anahita glanced over her shoulder to see who stood behind.

She was alone. This was herself. The new Anahita. 'Oh! Oh!' Trying to hold back her tears, she saw the broken brown teeth and yellowed eyes half hidden by wrinkles.

She turned away. Her knees were stiff, her back ached. A dirty stick provided something to lean on. With difficulty she picked the scarlet shoes from the dung-trodden earth and made her way from the yard.

Zohak Ali distributed coins to low-life beggars in the market. 'Anahita, the daughter of Kashgar the shoemaker, has been killed by an ugly old woman,' he told them. 'She has stolen her clothes and hidden the body where no one will find it. Spread the word through the city. But remember,' he raised a finger, 'if any one of you so much as mentions that we have spoken, I shall plague you *all* with broken bones and you will die in the gutters.'

The beggars shrank back, clutching their coins. 'We won't, Excellency . . . Your Highness . . . most Exalted One.'

'For I will *know*,' the magician told them. 'Now, be about your business.'

They scuttled away.

'What have you done with Anahita?' Fatima seized the ancient crone by the hair.

'Mother, I *am* Anahita.' She struggled free. 'How often do I have to tell you? I was on my way to—'

'Anahita? You are mad. How can you be my beautiful daughter? You are old enough to be my own grandmother.'

'I keep trying to tell—'

* * . * . * *. . * * * . * . * *. . * * *. . * . * 33 * * * . * . * *. . : * . * . * .

'I know who you are,' Fatima cried. 'The whole city is talking about it. You're a wandering gypsy. And you've killed my daughter!'

'Will you listen!' Anahita's voice was a parrot screech. 'Your name is Fatima. My brother's Farraj. He's fifteen years old. He has a little scar on his hand from when—'

'Aahhh! How do you know these things? Did you torture her? You devil!' Wet with tears, Fatima snatched up a cooking pot and struck the old woman about the head. 'Where is my daughter?'

Anahita put up her hands to defend herself.

'When my husband and son get back they will kill you!'

Frightened by her mother's violence, Anahita beat a retreat through the shop and out into the street.

'There she is, the murderess!' shouted some boys. They began to pelt her with stones.

An old man came to his door. 'What's happening?'

'This ugly old woman killed Anahita and stole her clothes,' a boy told him.

'Killed Anahita?' said the old man. 'Oh, you evil old witch!' He flung a broken horseshoe.

It hit Anahita on the head and she fell.

A crowd gathered. 'Murderer!' they shouted. 'Monster! Assassin!'

She pulled herself to her feet and began to stumble along the road. Handfuls of dirt spattered her face, sharp stones cut her back and legs. A dozen wounds began to bleed.

High in his blue tower, Zohak Ali looked down on his handiwork and laughed.

'Kill her!' the mob cried. 'Crush her! Burn her! Stone her from the city!'

And, in the absence of a body, that is what they did. Poor Anahita, clinging to the stick from the camel yard to prevent herself from falling, was beaten to the eastern gate. Four men grabbed her by the clothes and bore her through the entrance. 'There,' cried one, 'think yourself lucky.' Headlong they flung her to the stony ground. 'And don't come back.'

Anahita dragged herself to her feet. Painfully she hobbled away. A few last shouts and rocks pursued her from the city. The heavy gate slammed shut.

The Cave and
the Hawk

Heartbroken and hurting all over, Anahita made
her way from Samarkand. At her back the sun, a scarlet
ball, sank behind the golden domes and palaces that
rose above the city walls. Ahead lay the pink-lit summits
of the Pamirs.

Darkness forced her to halt. She crawled beneath a
thorn bush to get a little protection from the cold
night air. Whichever way she lay, her bones ached.
Long past midnight, clutching the clothes to her
throat, Anahita lay unsleeping. A snake slithered across
her foot. It was no worse than her thoughts: her poor
parents and Farraj and Prince Sohrab who would speak
to her no more, and the wickedness of Zohak Ali in his
fine Blue Palace.

What was to become of her? Banished from the city,
where could she go? If she were to survive she must

have shelter, food and water, and a fire. The best place for shelter, she thought, would be a cave in the mountains. For food she could pick berries and trap small animals. For fire she could spin a stick.

At first light, hungry and thirsty, she resumed her hobbling journey to the east. It took fourteen days but at last, high in the mountains and utterly exhausted, she discovered the cave that was to be her home for the next two years.

After she had chased out the bats and swept the floor clean, it was a perfect spot. Close at hand a trickle of sweet water ran down the rocks. An overhang gave protection to her fire. Dry grass made a comfortable bed. In the valley below there were berry bushes and some wild fruit trees. Fish swam in a stream. Bees had made honey in a rotted trunk.

The first weeks passed. Anahita looked like a wild woman: matted grey hair, broken nails and broken teeth, ragged clothes. But life and labour in the open air made her clear-eyed and vigorous, very different from the weary old creature Zohak Ali had conjured up. The wounds and bruises of the crowd soon healed. She experimented with herb poultices and the warts on her face disappeared. She sang favourite songs and invented new ones.

A thousand times she thought of her family and friends and sometimes wept. Had they forgotten her, she wondered; had this come true like the rest of the spell? There was no way of knowing. It was cruel. Sitting at the mouth of her cave she recalled the fire in her father's shop; and how Zohak Ali had turned the pedlar boy into a kitten and tried to kill it; and the many missing people, some of them her friends. Such wickedness was beyond her understanding. He would have to be stopped. Sultan Mushtaq, or the palace guard, or a party of brave men would have to *do* something before the city was completely in the magician's power.

But there was little time to brood. It was an hour-long descent into the valley where she fished and bathed. Wood had to be collected for the fire. Berries and leaves had to be gathered and her traps tended. The animals she caught had to be gutted, skinned and prepared for roasting on a spit or baking in clay. She needed a screen to deflect the wind which sometimes blew from snowfields. Her clothes had to be washed and repaired. She had to make shoes from skins. There was much to do.

And although there was not another person within fifty miles, she was far from alone. Throughout the long mountain days a family of little birds hopped about her cave entrance looking for seeds. A mouse made its home near her bed and crept towards the fire each evening for the warmth. Two frogs inhabited a tiny pool beneath her water supply.

Then there was Rosh.

*

It was late morning, cooler in the mountains than down on the plain, and Anahita had climbed to the top of a nearby hill. It had rained in the night, and as she lowered her head to drink from a pool she saw her reflection. It troubled her less where there was no one to see. She was used to it, yet it tugged her heart to remember Zohak Ali's prophecy. He was right, Prince Sohrab would never halt his horse to speak to a woman so old and ugly.

She sighed and sat back. Miles away and far below, a camel train wound through the mountains. It followed the Silk Road from China to Samarkand and on to India.

Her attention was distracted by the harsh cry of a bird. Anahita looked up and saw a flutter among rocks and tangled branches. She went to look. An enormous hawk, brown and speckled and gold, was trapped by the leg. With pitiless eyes it regarded her as she came close. It called again, *Ky-ow*, and fluttered its wings as if to pull the leg free. But one wing was broken and trailed towards the ground.

'Oh, you poor thing!' Anahita crouched beside it but not too close, for the hawk's hooked beak and talons could have ripped her flesh in a second. She extended a hand. The hawk watched intently but made no move to hurt her. With the back of a finger she stroked the soft plumage of its breast. The hawk's eyes double-blinked. She slid her hand towards its feathered legs. Her face was so close that the hawk could have struck at her eyes but it didn't. The wild creature seemed to understand that she wanted to help. Perhaps, even, its cry and flutter had been an appeal.

With care, old Anahita worked its leg loose and lifted the hawk to a bone-white branch where it could face the wind. The sad wing drooped. If she was to attempt to set it and look after the hawk while it recovered, she needed to carry it down to her cave.

How was this to be accomplished? She had seen the Sultan ride out with his falcon on his wrist. Anahita tore a strip from the hem of her dress and wrapped her wrist tightly. Gently she coaxed the injured hawk from its branch. Its talons dug through the cloth and stabbed her skin. It was sore. She gritted her teeth. Supporting her wrist with the other hand, Anahita started down the mountain.

Once at the cave, she set the hawk on a rock and scrubbed her wrist in the clear water. Then she pulled a handful of whippy grasses and peeled a strong, straight twig. 'This is going to hurt,' she said and felt for the break in the bone. The hawk watched her with yellow eyes. As the ends of bone grated together it gave a little *peep!* and made to snatch at her fingers but stopped short. She poked the grasses between its feathers and tied the twig tightly to its wing. The hawk pecked at it briefly and looked away.

Anahita rigged up a perch at the cave mouth and went to check her traps on the mountainside. They were empty but on the way back she nearly trod on a

cobra. She killed it with a stone and cut off its head. The starving hawk gripped the snake in its talons and tore it to pieces with its strong beak.

Anahita loved the fierce bird — though the mouse and frogs felt differently. She called it Rosh and they sat together blinking in the firelight.

In a month the bone was healed. As he sat on his perch, Rosh tested his great wings and was ready to lift into the wind. So Anahita, dreading to lose her friend, untied the grasses from his splint. With a tremendous sweep and his wild cry, *Ky-ow, Ky-ow*, Rosh launched into the air and sailed off across the valley. Half thrilled and half in tears, Anahita watched until he was a tiny speck above the snowy peaks of the Pamirs, then turned back into her cave.

He did not return that night, nor the next, but late in the afternoon of the third day, with a batter of wings and rush of air, he alighted in the cave mouth. In his talons was a mountain hare, freshly killed and still warm. Anahita was delighted. She lifted Rosh to his old perch. All she had to eat was a small fish which she had caught that morning and planned to cook for her evening meal. Sometimes Rosh liked fish. She gave it to him. Rosh played with it for a while, pecked here and there then threw it aside. But when Anahita gutted the hare and gave him the liver and lights, he gobbled them down then preened for half an hour and went to sleep.

*

Winter came with snow and hunger.

Then blazing summer.

Another winter.

Another summer.

A score of times Anahita planned to make the journey home but somehow the days and weeks slipped by. Things could never be as they had been. Did she really want to swap her simple life for the crowds and perils of the city? It was many miles. What would she find when she got there? Perhaps she would be recognized and thrown into jail – or even worse.

Had she been unhappy in the mountains she would have gone long before. But once she had grown used to it, there was much to enjoy in the life of a hermit. She loved her cave, her wild companions, the dramatic scenery, the river where she fished and swam, the spectacular storms, sunrise and moonlight, the little garden she made of wild flowers. Had she been undisturbed, there is no knowing how long she might have remained.

But early one evening an event occurred which was to shatter the peace of her mountain days and send Anahita back to the dangers of Samarkand.

It was two hours to sunset. The rocks were warm and she sat in the mouth of the cave stitching skins with gut and a bone needle to make a coat for the coming winter. Far beneath her a caravan wound along the Silk Road. She paused to watch – then stiffened.

Visible to her but hidden from the camel drivers, a group of bandits had set an ambush.

There was nothing she could do. The caravan came on. The bandits swept down from their place of hiding. There was fierce fighting and slaughter. Even from where she stood, Anahita heard the distant screams and saw the red. It did not last long. Leaving the drivers where they lay to be eaten by wild animals and vultures, the bandits rounded up the camels and turned from the Silk Road to passes through the mountains.

The route was steep and Anahita was alarmed to discover it led towards her cave. For the first time in two years she doused her fire. The sun set but enough light remained for her to see the wolfish bandits as they passed not a hundred metres distant. They were laughing and drinking, clothes stained with blood – all but the leader who rode apart. She caught words: '. . . mad Chinese Emperor to the Caliph of Baghdad . . . never seen treasure like this lot . . . deserve a bigger share.'

Unseen by the rest, a man slipped his hand into one of the panniers. The leader dropped back. A scimitar flashed. The man's arm was chopped off at the elbow. He screamed.

The leader said, 'I warned you.'

He rode a white camel. His robes were black. A diamond big as a goose egg flashed from his turban.

It was Zohak Ali.

*

The robbers passed on.

What was the magician doing there, Anahita wondered, then realized that he must have known this was a treasure-laden caravan. But why had he not used his magic to stop the camel drivers resisting? Perhaps he liked being with the wild bandits. Perhaps he enjoyed killing.

She shivered and examined her fire. By good luck a spark of red remained. She coaxed it into flame and cooked her evening meal.

The frogs croaked. The stars came out. Mouse and his little family crept towards the fire.

Anahita looked at her old hands. She thought: if I stay in the mountains much longer I will die here. It is time to return to the city. I will hide my face. I will find some place to live, and work to earn money to buy food. I will get news of my father and mother and Farraj. And Prince Sohrab. I will discover what wickedness Zohak Ali has been conjuring. He has ruined my life, and the life of that poor pedlar boy, and the families of all those merchants and drivers lying dead on the Silk Road. If there is anything an old woman can do to stop him, I must try.

During the next few days she made her preparations. Her thick grey hair trailed far down her back; with a sharp stone she chopped it shorter. Using grasses and her own hair for thread, she repaired the rips in her clothing. For the last time she swam in her pool in the valley. She said goodbye to the little birds and the family of mice and the frogs. And one morning she left the cave that had been her home for two whole years and commenced the long journey back to Samarkand. High overhead, Rosh sailed against the blue.

The Swineherd

While Anahita lived in the mountains, Samarkand had suffered many changes.

Sultan Mushtaq was a gentle ruler, loved throughout the city. For half a century he had maintained the law by a benign justice and the support of his people. When a ravening wolf like Zohak Ali came among them, he was unprepared. The palace guard, a ceremonial body in handsome uniforms, was sent against the magician, but what could soldiers do when they were turned to men of straw, what use were scimitars when they turned to feathers? The Sultan confronted Zohak Ali, man to man, but the magician just laughed. And when Prince Sohrab went missing along with so many other citizens, Mushtaq was broken-hearted. Black bows were tied around the palm trees and he retreated inside his palace to care for his wives and younger children.

Zohak Ali, in contrast, was fully prepared and leaped into the vacuum the Sultan's absence left at the heart of the city's rule. He established an army of tax collectors and increased the rents and taxes tenfold. He trebled the number of spies who slid like snakes through the alleys and kept him informed of every whisper of resistance. He emptied the vaults of Sultan Mushtaq, seized the possessions of the richest merchants, stripped the sheaths of beaten gold from the domes of the mosques, robbed the churches of their treasures, even forced poor widows to sell their sticks of furniture to pay his demands. Any citizen who refused was visited by Zohak's police, a ruthless gang in red robes with daggers in their belts and clubs in their hands. He did not resist for long when he was savagely beaten and his children had knives put to their throats.

The city was driven to its knees.

At the same time, in his secret caves beneath the Blue Palace, the heaps of gold and white skulls of the magician's enemies mounted towards the roof.

Part of the treasure he used to equip an army and send his generals off into neighbouring regions: west to Bukhara, north to Tashkent, south into Persia and Kashmir. Their raids were bloody and successful. Still more wealth flooded back to Samarkand. Traders carried tales along the Silk Road into China and India. Though it was early days, the name of Zohak Ali was being spoken across Asia.

*

Anahita walked the streets. For days she could find neither work nor shelter. Boys shouted after her. Women drew their skirts aside as she passed. Nobody was interested in a strange old creature who hid her face and mended her rags with grass. She slept beneath a cart in the market square and ate what the traders tipped out at the end of the day.

The influence of Zohak Ali was all about her. The alleys were alive with stray dogs and starving mules. It had long been known that anyone who angered or hindered the magician was removed with a spell. People had seen it: one second Rashid was there, the next a mangy mongrel was scuttling along the street; one moment Yasmin stood crying, the next she had vanished and a buzzing fly landed on her father's turban. The city was afraid: dare they kill this cockroach? Is this flea-ridden donkey really my mother?

Words had been chalked on the walls, something no one had ever seen in Samarkand:

Have you seen a stray yak?
Contact Hassan the tailor.

Help the hungry.

Zohak Ali must be destroyed.

Anahita had been frightened that when she returned to the city she would be recognized. Now she realized that so much had happened, so many lives had been devastated, that no one cared about, no one even remembered, the pretty daughter of Kashgar, the shoemaker, or the old woman who was said to have killed her.

Every day she went to her father's workshop. He was never there. Neither was Farraj. The shop looked abandoned. One day, through an open door, she saw a frail stranger in the room beyond. Anahita looked more closely. It was her mother. The merry Fatima had lost her plump arms, lost her laughter. Her black, black hair had turned snow white. With hunched shoulders she sat on a box. Tears dripped to the dusty floor.

After a week Anahita found work in pigsties a short distance from the walls of the Blue Palace. The owner was a rough, unpleasant fellow who would have preferred a man. The pigs were thin, the sties broken and filthy. A little house, in similar condition, went with the job.

It was hard work for anyone, let alone a woman as old as Anahita, but life in the mountains had made her strong. Day by day she repaired the sties, shovelled out the muck and replaced it with fresh straw, scrubbed the troughs and filled them with whey and stalks and grain. The pigs thrived and greeted her when she went into the sties, jostling to have their backs scratched.

Her wages were tiny but it cost nothing to clean the two rooms of her house and little more to obtain a few fragments of quicklime which she crushed to make whitewash. Soon the little house gleamed, inside and out. The roof leaked in one or two places when it rained but it didn't matter, there was nothing to spoil. The water ran straight through the floor into the ground and when the sun came out, the boards were dry in an hour.

Rosh remained in the mountains but often came to visit. Sometimes he stayed for two or three days. Anahita fixed up a shelf for him just inside an open window. She bought scrag-ends of meat but there was no need, for Rosh found plenty to eat beyond the city walls. In fact, he was the better provider, for often he brought her a juicy rabbit or a partridge, fresh from a hillside twenty miles away. Sometimes he carried a hen, snatched from a run within the city. Anahita hid it away quickly until it was safe to pluck it and put it in the pot. The thought did cross her mind that this might not always have been a hen, but the same could be said of every chicken in the market and she was hungry, so she ate it anyway.

Her little house had a second inhabitant, a yellow lizard who moved in and established himself after a few days. He lived in a hole at the bottom of the wall and could go anywhere, up the walls, down the walls, across the ceiling. Anahita liked to watch him stalking the fat flies that came in from the pigsties. One foot at a time he crept nearer and nearer, froze, then with a flick of his tongue, too fast to see, the fly was gone and he was chomping his lizard jaws, legs and wings sticking out all round. He was quite tame and in the evenings, except when Rosh was in residence, he climbed on to the arm of her rickety chair and she fed him tiny scraps of meat. She called him Lizard.

A fever rampaged through the city and Anahita became ill. For a day she managed to look after the pigs but when she returned home she was so weak that she fell to the floor.

'No work, no wages,' the pig owner told her the next day. 'You can stay in the house till you're better but someone's got to look after the sties. I've found a boy. You're sacked.'

This was serious. Anahita needed medicines which took every penny of her tiny savings. The fever tightened its grip. For weeks she hardly knew if it was day or night. Many people in the city died. Anahita thought that she, too, was going to die but in the end she began to feel a little stronger. Then she needed food: not the dead fur and feathers that Rosh carried from the mountains but fruit and milk and more medicines, for she was still a very sick old lady. The fever had taken its toll: her eyes had lost their sparkle, her ribs stood out, her arms were so weak that she could hardly raise them. Had she fought off the fever, she thought, only to die of starvation?

The pig owner came again. 'Still here? What are you going to do, get better or die? Make up your mind. I'm wanting the house.'

*

Lizard came out of his hole. Wearily Anahita turned her head and watched as he ran across the bare boards. His energy made her smile. Something was in his mouth, something as bright as himself. He jumped to the bed and climbed across the cover. The thing fell by her hand. She picked it up and stared. It was a gold coin. Where had Lizard got a gold coin? Head on one side, eyes bright as jewels, he looked at her.

'Oh, you lovely, clever Lizard!' Anahita said.

For several minutes she lay gathering her strength then made her way along the wall to the window. A boy was sweeping the street. She gave him the coin and he ran off to buy oranges, dates, bread, medicines and a treat for himself. As she sat on the bed to await his return, Anahita began to think that perhaps she would get better.

The money lasted three days. Anahita made slow progress. She could wash and walk across the room. Her head began to clear.

The fourth day dawned. As she peeled the last of the oranges and picked the last crumbs from her plate, Anahita wondered what she would eat that evening – and the next day, and the next. She looked around her bare room. There was nothing to sell: a blanket, a chipped cup, a cooking pot. She closed her eyes.

And while she slept in her broken chair, grey hair straggling over her shoulders, a remarkable thing happened. Lizard emerged from his hole with another gold coin in his mouth. He dropped it on the floor and ran

back. A while later he emerged with a second. And then a third. A careless cockroach caught his attention. He stalked it across the wall, crunched it up with lizard enjoyment, and flickered back into his hole.

It was the chink of a coin, a long time later, that roused Anahita from her sleep. Drowsily she looked around and saw the little heap of coins on the floorboards. The tip of Lizard's tail vanished from sight.

Anahita could not believe it. She counted: twelve gold coins! She could buy all the food she needed. Buy clothes and throw away her pig-smelling rags. Pay rent to the owner and not be thrown out on the street. She was saved.

'Oh, you wonderful, wonderful Lizard!' she called to the hole in the wall.

It was a miracle. But how did Lizard know she needed it? Mouse in the mountains was a mouse. The frogs were frogs. But Lizard brought her gold coins. Ate squashy bluebottles and saved her life.

Rosh swept to the window ledge. A fat duck fell from his talons. Anahita thought that in a day or so she might be ready to cook it.

'And you, my beautiful,' she said and stroked his soft feathers with the back of her fingers.

Rosh blinked his fierce golden eyes and nibbled the crown of her head with his deadly beak.

But Lizard was not finished. All that day, and night, and the next, and the next, he ran to and fro. The pile of coins grew bigger and bigger. Where was he getting them?

Anahita puzzled. No one in that neighbourhood had so much money. Perhaps he had discovered a cache of buried treasure. Or perhaps— She looked from the window. Hillsides rose above the nearby houses. She bent to see the towering walls of the Blue Palace on the summit. Could he be stealing them from Zohak Ali himself? Surely not, the palace was well guarded and too far away.

Wherever they came from, Anahita was rich. Though an old woman, she recovered from the fever and grew healthy and strong again. She bought her house from the vile owner and bought the pig farm too and engaged a kindly man who would treat the animals well. She bought fine clothes and tipped the beggars and ruined merchants who approached her in the street.

Who was this mysterious veiled lady who had come among them, the city wondered. This lady who was as kind as Zohak Ali was cruel. Why did she not buy a better house? What had become of the queer old pig woman in rags?

Fatima's Story

One morning, as the streets steamed after a shower of rain, Anahita saw a figure she thought she recognized. She looked closer. It was her mother, white-haired Fatima. Her clothes were wet. A sickle hung from one hand and she was bowed beneath a heavy bale of grass. Anahita was heartbroken. That her poor mother should be reduced to labouring in the streets!

That same evening she paid her mother a visit. Smells of cooking drifted from the windows of other houses. She knocked on the workshop door.

Fatima carried a candle and was startled to see her rich, veiled visitor. She salaamed. 'May I be of assistance?'

Anahita saw her mother's work-worn face and roughened hands, the stained folds of her dress. Tears ran down her cheeks and for a moment she could not speak.

'What is it brings your ladyship to a house as humble as my own?' said Fatima.

'I am new to the city,' Anahita said at length. 'I wonder, would you be kind enough to allow me to enter for a moment? Oh!' She made a pretence of feeling faint.

'You are not well.' Fatima took her elbow. 'Here, let me help you.' She guided Anahita through the doorway.

The flickering candle threw light over the workshop. It had been stripped of all the tools and equipment, the shelves stood empty.

'You are welcome but I am afraid it is a poor home.' Fatima led the way. 'Times are hard.'

'Indeed the city is troubled.' As Anahita followed her mother into the room where she had passed her childhood, she could hardly refrain from crying out. The grate stood empty. The furniture, the rugs, the small embroideries, everything she had known and loved was gone.

'Please sit down.' Fatima offered her the only chair. 'Can I fetch you some water?'

'No, thank you. A seat is all I need, just for a moment.'

Fatima busied herself with an oil lamp.

The glass funnel was broken. As it burned up, she saw her guest looking round the bare walls. A gaudy portrait of Zohak Ali hung above the fireplace, his eyes fierce, beard thrusting, the Bangalore diamond flashing in his turban.

'Everybody must have one of those,' said Fatima. 'It's the new law. Inspectors come round. If they don't see it on display you get beaten.' She followed Anahita's gaze and was embarrassed. 'We had a comfortable home, a happy home, though you wouldn't think so to see it now.'

'My dear, tell me,' said Anahita. 'What happened?'

'Oh, it's a long story, common enough in the city these days.' Fatima sat on a low, three-legged stool. 'My husband was a shoemaker—'

'Was?' Anahita was chilled.

'You may have heard of him, Kashgar al Kharif. He was quite well known.'

'Yes, indeed.' Anahita struggled with her feelings. 'I had a pair of his slippers myself at one time. They were much admired.' She remembered that she was recently arrived in Samarkand. 'They were a gift.'

'They found their way to many cities.' Fatima smiled. 'Well, one day he sent our daughter, the most beautiful girl you ever saw,' she touched her white hair, 'to deliver a pair of red shoes. She never returned. People say she was killed by a hideous old woman. It broke my husband's heart. He could not rest from searching for her. Then one evening he, too, disappeared. He had gone to the Blue Palace – at least that's what my handsome, lovely son, Farraj, told me.'

'Why to the Blue Palace?'

'You must have heard.' Fatima lowered her voice. 'Everything wicked and cruel and mysterious starts up there. Samarkand was a happy city before Zohak Ali came here and built his palace.' She pointed to the window where the roofs and tower of the Blue Palace were silhouetted against the stars.

'Oh, Fath—' Anahita checked herself. 'So your husband went up there and never came back?'

'My son, too, Farraj. Young, hot-blooded. He worshipped his father.' Fatima's voice broke. 'Nothing I could say would stop him. Went off one morning, striding up the hill with a sword at his belt. I never saw him again.'

'Poor Farraj!'

'Why, did you know him?' Fatima looked at her visitor sharply.

'No, I was just thinking. Your husband, your son.'

'Oh, they're not the only ones went up there. A score, two score. Prince Sohrab was one of the first – you know, Sultan Mushtaq's son.'

Anahita repressed a cry.

'All in white with his golden turban,' Fatima continued. 'On his white stallion. Rode right through the entrance, calling on Zohak Ali to come out and face him.'

'What happened?'

'The horse got away, or so I've heard. Galloping and bleeding. Clawed by those big cats he keeps up there. Prince Sohrab – nobody knows what happened.'

'How horrible!' Anahita tried to stifle her imagination. 'Did nobody ever come out?'

'There was one man, a professor from the university. But they say he'd gone mad, staring and gibbering. He had to be locked away in the asylum.'

Anahita longed to hug her mother. Instead she said, 'What about you?'

'Me?' Fatima wiped her eyes. 'I searched and searched but nobody knew anything. No one could help. Who can blame them, they have troubles enough of their own.'

'But how do you live, now you have no husband and your children are gone?'

'As I say, we had a comfortable home. But I can't make shoes and—' She broke off. A rat had appeared by the empty fireplace. 'Go on, disgusting, dirty—' She snatched a spoon from the orange box which served as a table and threw it. The spoon hit the rat on the tail. With a squeak it ran away.

'Filthy thing!' Fatima said. 'It's got a hole out in the workshop. The city's getting infested. If my husband were here it wouldn't last long, he'd buy poison or set a trap.' She had become agitated. 'I can't stand them!'

'But you were saying.' Anahita steered her back. 'You're alone now and you can't make shoes.'

'Well, I can't.' Fatima fanned the neck of her dress for air. 'What do I know about lasts and leather and all the rest of it? But I have to eat. So little by little I've had to sell things in the market until — well, you see.'

She gestured to the empty room. 'Now I work for a camel driver by the South Gate.'

'I have seen you in the street,' Anahita said. 'It's hard work.'

'If only that were all,' said Fatima. 'He wants to marry me, then he need pay me nothing at all. As if I would marry a mean, disgusting, foul-mouthed beast like that!'

'If you will let me,' Anahita said, 'perhaps I can help you. To be honest, it's why I am here.'

'You have news about my husband?'

'Unfortunately no. But I am a wealthy woman. When I saw you, with your kind face, struggling beneath a load no woman should have to carry, I realized how easy it would be for me to lift it from your shoulders.'

Anahita slipped a hand into her pocket and withdrew a small leather pouch. She pressed it into her mother's fingers.

'Here, please take it. I want no thanks. You would do me an honour.'

Fatima was struck dumb. She stared from her veiled visitor to the washleather bag in her hand. With fumbling fingers she untied the string. Within was the glint of gold. She tipped it into her hand. A coin fell to the floor. She picked it up.

'Oh, your ladyship! How kind! How kind!'

She straightened and turned to her visitor.

But Anahita was gone.

Fatima ran out into the street. Her saviour had disappeared.

Anahita hid in a doorway until her mother had returned into the house then went on her way. As she walked through the starlit city, still weary from her illness and leaning heavily on a cane, she realized that something had to be done — she had no idea what but something — to stop this man who had destroyed her family and caused so much more misery besides.

Every day as she grew stronger, she learned of fresh outrages. Houses had been seized and given to spies; pets fed to the tigers; camels crippled so that Zohak Ali's entries won every race.

The more she heard, the more angry she became. Anahita racked her brains. *What* could be done to rid the city of this ruthless magician?

At last she had an idea.

Poisoned Wine

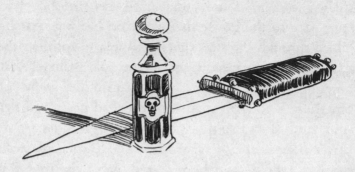

Anahita engaged a gardener, a builder and two artists to make changes to her little abode. She gave them precise instructions.

The men worked hard. The gardener fenced off an area and planted it with beautiful shrubs and flowers. The builder repaired the roof, walls and window shutters and laid new floors. The artists painted every centimetre, outside and in. One room they covered with an intricate design in gold and crimson, the other they painted white. The white room they furnished with a cool white table, two white chairs and floating curtains to keep out the glare. The crimson room they enriched with a large Bukhara rug, tapestries, silk brocade ottomans and a beautiful inlaid table. There were vases, carvings, a green jade cat. Flowers filled the air with perfume.

While all this was taking place, Anahita visited the last remaining dressmaker in Samarkand, who before the arrival of Zohak Ali had been dressmaker to the Sultan's wives, and was measured for the wardrobe of a rich lady.

She engaged a poor but well-spoken boy to be her house-servant and dressed him in livery.

Finally she made two purchases. In a little shop she bought a pointed and very sharp fruit knife. And from an apothecary in a narrow back street she obtained a phial of deadly poison – and the antidote.

Anahita was ready to set her plan in motion.

Accompanied by her young servant, she visited the room of an amanuensis, a man who earned his living by writing letters for people who could neither read nor write. Anahita could do both, though not very well. She told the man what she wanted: a card inviting Zohak Ali, Lord of the Blue Palace, to dine with a wealthy widow recently arrived in Samarkand. A man as wicked and detestable as Zohak Ali, she realized, was very likely lonely, despite his beautiful surroundings. Moreover, he was obsessively greedy and the thought of robbing a rich and helpless widow would be irresistible.

The card was soon written, a work of art with many curlicues. Anahita paid the amanuensis and dispatched her reluctant servant to the Blue Palace.

He was back within the hour. Zohak Ali would be pleased to accept the invitation.

She had three days to complete her preparations.

Rosh — and when Rosh was not there, Lizard — watched the comings and goings with interest. Goblets and plates were delivered. The finest wines. And food: quails' eggs, pigeon breasts, fish roe, spiced meats, wild duck, white mullet, venison in aspic, freshwater mussels, suckling pig, five kinds of rice — the quantities were modest, the variety great. All these, with burners to keep the food hot, would be served in the rich room.

For the white room Anahita ordered the wine to be chilled, salted almonds, ginger, cheeses, fruits — mangoes, fresh figs, lychees, muskmelon, peeled grapes, pomegranates, kumquats, sugared limes, glazed strawberries — and coffee.

It was very expensive. By the time she had finished, all that remained of Lizard's shining store, hidden beneath a loosened floorboard, were three gold coins.

It did not matter, her preparations were complete. It only remained to await the hour.

A little before sunset Anahita dressed in her finest. Even though her face would be hidden, she anointed her eyes with belladonna and kohl, her lips and cheeks with rouge. She slipped rings on to her gnarled fingers.

As the sky turned bloodshot, she tipped the phial of deadly poison into the red wine in the rich room, and placed the knife by the bowls of fruit in the white room where she could snatch it up in a second.

Minutes later she heard footsteps and a firm rap at the door. There were voices then her trembling servant announced: 'Lord Zohak Ali is here, my lady.'

He was an even more frightening figure than she remembered. Fresh murders and power had added to his presence. His black eyes burned; the cruel lines in his cheeks were deeper; his hands glittered with jewels the size of pigeon eggs. For the evening his robes were dark and richly ornamented. The Bangalore diamond flashed fire from his turban.

'I am honoured you accept my humble invitation, sir.' Anahita bowed gracefully.

'Much is spoken in the city about the veiled lady who spends so freely,' he replied.

'Much, too, about the great Zohak Ali,' she said. 'Lord of the magnificent Blue Palace. Whose armies make conquests on every side.'

He acknowledged her words and took the seat she offered. 'So you are newly come to Samarkand?'

'Indeed, sir. From Bokhara, Cairo, Constantinople,' said Anahita who had never in her life, except for her sojourn in the mountains, travelled beyond the city. She had, however, spent many hours struggling to understand books about these places in the library at the university. 'I travel much.'

'I lived in Constantinople myself for some time,' said Zohak Ali. 'I liked to take my coffee at one of those tables by the Mosque of Ahmed — you must know it — and watch the ships coming through the Golden Horn.'

'You confuse me, sir. Surely the great Mosque of Ahmed is in the south of the city and the Golden Horn is in the north.'

'Ah, yes. You are right. It is some years.' Zohak Ali sat forward. 'But tell me, may a guest enquire why you go about Samarkand, and your house, so heavily veiled?'

Anahita bowed her head.

'You are a lady of mystery. The city is intrigued. From what I learn, no one has ever seen your face.'

'Nor will they, sir,' said Anahita. 'For I was disfigured when I was a child. A cauldron spilled over my face. My features are not such as I wish any man to look upon.' She straightened and rose. 'But come, to more lively matters. Would your honour care to join me at the table?' She gestured to the feast. 'I have been to only the best suppliers. The food is fresh. I trust you will find it to your liking.'

'Thank you. My appetite returns with the cool of evening.' Zohak Ali stroked his beard and took the chair she indicated.

Anahita sat opposite and rang a little bell. Her servant appeared. 'Some wine for Lord Zohak,' she said.

The boy, who knew nothing about the poison, had been carefully coached. He filled the glass with wine, red as a ruby which burned on the magician's breast. From the same earthenware flagon he filled Anahita's glass also. For her plan was to toast her guest and, if necessary, drink with him lest he became suspicious. The phial of antidote nestled safely in her pocket.

'With what can I tempt your lordship's palate?' she said. 'Oysters, to begin? Baikal caviar? A little mullet?'

He surveyed the table. 'Kedgeree, I think.'

Good, thought Anahita. Good. The spice would disguise any bitterness in the wine, though the apothecary had assured her there would be none.

But Zohak Ali was cunning. He had not deceived, murdered and ridden roughshod over powerful men without making enemies. There had been many attempts on his life. This wealthy old woman: her offer had been tempting – too tempting. She would be easy to outwit – too easy. Her history, her travels, her disfigurement, her veils, they were intriguing – too intriguing. He slipped a hand, unseen, into one of a number of small purses at his waist and withdrew a pinch of powdered wasp wings mixed with mandragora. Choosing the moment when the servant boy was bending above the kedgeree, he blew it across the table. Instantly Anahita and the boy fell into a trance. The little cloud floated in the air. The plates of food were unaltered. But in the crimson heart of the wine, in each glass and a drip that clung to the lip of the flagon, a death's-head glowed. With a grin it invited them to its burning kingdom.

Zohak Ali smiled back.

The cloud settled and vanished. The glow faded.

The boy resumed serving kedgeree.

Anahita raised her glass. 'To you, my lord. To your health and prosperity, the continued success of your camels.'

'And to you, my mysterious hostess. May long life be yours.' He raised the glass to his lips, seemed about to drink, then set it down. 'Alas, no.' He fanned his cheeks. 'Suddenly I have no appetite for hot food. Do I see fruit and cooling wine beyond the curtain?'

Anahita was aghast. With an effort she maintained her composure. 'You are certain? The food is good, the wine is from the best vineyards.'

'Yes, indeed. I pray you take no offence.' He swallowed two oysters and popped a quail's egg into his mouth.

Anahita rose, relieved that at least she need not put the antidote to the test, and led the way from her richly-furnished room.

White walls, white flowers and space made the adjoining room cool. The green jade Siamese cat stood on a shelf; a single African mask broke the bareness of the walls. On the white table the fruits and ginger glowed like jewels.

The magician sat and the boy poured wine. He offered figs and limes. Zohak Ali put out a hand. At that instant, before he could select, Anahita snatched up the fruit knife and struck a ferocious blow at the magician's heart.

He would have been slain on the spot but the Devil

looks after his own. Anahita's outer sleeve caught on a corner of the table. Her hand fell short. And before she could strike again, Zohak Ali knocked the two plates of food into her face and sprang away.

His chair fell.

The servant boy screamed and ran from the house.

Anahita leaped forward. Her hood and veils fell back.

But now the magician was ready for her. 'Stop!'

Her legs struck an invisible wall. Her feet felt gripped by a vice. Anahita struggled to stab at him but could not reach.

He plucked a lemon from the table and held it towards her. 'Eat!'

Unable to help herself, she took the sour fruit and bit into it. The juice burned her mouth. Her eyes watered. She munched.

'Biter bit and bitter bite,
Shrink and shrivel, blast and blight!'

Zohak Ali flung both arms above his head.

Anahita swallowed the crunchy mouthful. Instantly, as if it were poison, her whole body was seized by a convulsion. The room seemed to crash about her. The world turned to chaos. And when it stilled, Anahita found herself shrunk to the length of a lady's finger. She was still old, nothing had changed, except that she was now tiny. The chairs and table towered overhead.

Zohak Ali was the height of a mountain. He looked down and laughed, a sound like thunder.

'So, shoemaker's daughter. The mysterious old woman was you. I should have guessed. But where have you been since that afternoon in the camel yard; since I watched them stone you from the East Gate? Where did *you* get so much money?' He crouched beside her. 'Will you tell me or shall I squash you like a little grey mouse? Drop you from a great height?'

Anahita backed away. He put out finger and thumb to pick her up by the dress. He should have been more cautious, she still had the fruit knife. Like her clothes, it had shrunk with her. As the giant hand came towards her, adorned with jewels bigger than her head, she drew back the knife and plunged it into his thumb.

Zohak Ali roared and sprang to his feet. A drop of blood, big as a puddle, splashed to the floor. She ran for cover. The magician raised his foot to stamp on her. Anahita dodged aside. He stamped again. She found safety beneath the white table. He dragged back the fallen chair and flung a wine flagon. It exploded beside her. She ran through the flood, seeking shelter.

Zohak Ali looked around. The green jade cat stared into space. He made passes in the air, spoke magic words, blew towards it. The Siamese arched its back, stretched wicked claws and sprang to the floor. It spotted Anahita.

At the same instant Anahita saw a movement at the

foot of the wall. It was the yellow lizard, dancing by his hole to gain her attention. She raced towards it.

The cat was faster. In a moment it was at her back. A paw trapped the sweeping hem of her dress. She was stopped in her tracks. Anahita looked behind and saw the grass-green eyes, the cavernous red mouth fringed with needle-sharp teeth. The cat batted her aside. She was bowled over.

Again that thunderous noise of the magician's laughter.

Anahita picked herself up and ran on. The cat watched then made a pretty bound and caught her beside a table leg. It was playing with her. She tugged her skirt. It was held fast by those hooked claws.

Not for long. She raised her arm and stabbed the fruit knife handle-deep into the cat's paw. With an ear-splitting yowl the cat sprang back and tore around the room. Anahita did not pause to watch. Headlong she raced towards the lizard's hole.

A metre distant, hissing and spitting, the cat came to a halt. Zohak Ali ran round the table.

Right at the entrance Anahita tripped over her trailing dress and fell. The magician's shoe descended. She scrambled aside. The cat was upon her. Lizard emerged from his hole and clamped her dress in his mouth. He pulled. The cat struck out and tore the skirt to shreds. Zohak Ali, trying again to stamp on her, trod on the cat's tail. It gave a screech of rage and raked its claws down his leg.

Dragged by the lizard and scrambling on hands and knees, Anahita vanished into the hole.

He released her clothes and ran ahead into the darkness. Holding out her arms to protect her face, Anahita followed.

The Nest
Beneath the City

The lizard halted. Light came from a crack in the tunnel wall. There was a smell of ginger and baking bread. Anahita wondered where it could be coming from and remembered a little bakery just a minute's walk from her cottage. She sank to the ground. Lizard looked at her, head on one side, then darted away.

He was soon back, a big cake crumb in his mouth. He dropped it in her lap, smelling deliciously of cherries and orange. Anahita broke off a fragment and ate it. She stroked the top of the lizard's scaly head. 'Thank you, Lizard,' she said. 'You saved my life.'

Lizard blinked and smacked his mouth as if he was munching a fly then lay down at her side.

Back in her little house, meanwhile, Zohak Ali was in a fury. He turned the cat back into an ornament and smashed it to a thousand splinters. He threw over the fruit table and strode into the adjoining room. The glasses and flagons of blood-red wine exploded like bombs against the walls and furniture. Poison ran to the floor. He tore down the tapestries and raked the beautiful table with a corner of pottery.

His anger ran its course. He subsided on to an embroidered chair and examined the scratch in his leg. A few words eased the sting. The bleeding stopped. It began to heal over.

He sank back and relaxed. Where did the old woman keep her money? That, after all, was his reason for coming. That and curiosity. He smiled, it had been an interesting evening. Now — where?

The rich room revealed nothing, but the floor of the white room was sandalwood. He found the loose board in a corner. Beneath lay all that remained of Anahita's little hoard — three gold coins. He tipped them into his pocket and continued the search, certain there must be more. But there was not: prying fingers, eyes and magic could discover nothing. If not in the house, he wondered, where *was* the rest of her wealth? Where had it come from? Where had she been all that time? Cross at having no answers, he returned into the street. Behind him he left the door wide open and shouted into the velvet darkness: 'Help yourselves!'

It did not take long for the ne'er-do-wells who roamed the night to discover Anahita's lamplit entrance. The house was deserted. What an orgy of food and thieving! Swarming like ants, they crammed their mouths, became drunk on the remaining bottles of wine, scraped delicacies from the floor and sucked their fingers clean, bundled up Anahita's clothes, fought over the rugs, carried off the furniture and plates, even pulled up the floorboards and uprooted the bushes in the garden.

The last thief vanished into the sprawling city. Zohak Ali, watching from the shadows, laughed with satisfaction. Noiseless as a fox, he slipped away.

When all was quiet, Anahita and Lizard ventured from his hole. The devastation was complete. Nothing remained of her lovely house but four bare walls and a roof. The moon shone through a naked window. She had tried, she had done her best, but Zohak Ali had been too clever for her.

The tiny old lady turned to her companion. 'Well, what do we do now, Lizard?'

His eyes were bright in the moonlight. He opened his jaws as if he wished to speak then nudged her with his nose and turned back into the hole.

Anahita caught hold of the tip of his tail and followed.

Her house stood abandoned.

They walked for hours and began to climb. Lizard could have run ten times as fast but Anahita was blind in the darkness and tired. Passages, felt rather than seen, led off to right and left. For centuries the animals of Samarkand had been constructing a maze of tunnels. It was their thoroughfare, the equivalent of the streets and alleys in the city above. Wherever they wanted to go – to Kashgar's workshop or the Great Mosque or the palace of Sultan Mushtaq – there was a tunnel to take them there. Sounds penetrated from the world of men: footsteps, a driver shouting at his camel, a bump as something fell and showered them with grit. Lizard turned one way, then another. Anahita was completely lost. If he had deserted her she would have died down there, starved or become a meal for some passing snake or mongoose. She gripped his tail tight.

At last they reached Lizard's destination, a widening in the tunnel like a small midway chamber. He halted. Anahita groped on all sides and stumbled over something cold and metallic. She ignored it. To her left was the earth wall. To the right her hands encountered what felt like a comfortable bed of grass and bits of fluff and paper and a few curly feathers. It had a warm, welcoming smell. Lizard pushed her gently towards it.

'Oh, thank you, Lizard. Thank you!'

Anahita crawled over the edge into the middle of the bed or nest and curled up with her head on her hands. Briefly it occurred to her that it was a very big nest for Lizard but she was too tired to think about it. The only thing in the whole world she wanted at that moment was to close her eyes in the friendly dark and go to sleep.

So she did.

And as she slept, she was dimly aware of being moved, as her mother had moved her when she was a sleepy little girl. But this wasn't her mother, it was something big and snuffly and furry and warm. It curled around in the bed. Anahita buried her hands and face in its soft fur and slept on.

It was the deepest, sweetest, safest sleep she had known for a long time and when she woke it was daylight. Daylight outside, that is, for in the tunnel it was still dark, though a short distance from where she lay a narrow beam of sunlight pierced the gloom.

The creature at Anahita's side was grooming itself. It may have been the movement which woke her. She looked up at the black fur, a wall of fur much higher than herself, and wondered what it was. The next moment she knew. A whiskery face looked round at her, an intelligent face with black eyes, big ears and long front teeth. It was a rat.

Anahita was terrified. She sprang back and groped for her knife. It was lost somewhere in the big nest. She jumped to the ground and ran to the far side of the little chamber. Lizard was there. She clung to him for safety and looked back at the rat, big as an elephant.

Lizard was unafraid. Anahita did not know he had passed this way many times and knew the rat well.

The rat had stopped grooming and was looking at her. He didn't look in the least dangerous or savage. On the contrary, there was something almost sad in his

face. He sat up on his hind legs and scratched his soft belly with both paws. Anahita remembered him coming into the nest during the night and how safe and cosy she had felt. He had not hurt her then.

And while she stood wondering, the rat did a surprising thing. He jumped down from the nest and ran away up the tunnel. As he passed through the sunbeam his black coat sparkled with health, his bottom wiggled, his long tail trailed on the ground. A minute later he was back and although there was no avoiding the fact that he was a *rat*, Anahita had to admit that he was a fine fellow. He was carrying something in his mouth. It was a freshly picked grape. He dropped it before her, big as a barrel, and sat up on his tail. High overhead, his whiskery face looked down. The black eyes blinked. Nervously she stepped round the grape and touched his soft fur. He gave a little squeak of pleasure. A long paw with sharp claws hung by her head. Anahita reached up and took hold of it. 'Hello, Rat.' The rat was overwhelmed. Like a puppy whose owners have returned, he fell to four paws and scampered up the tunnel one way, down the other and bounded back, nudging her shoulder with his nose. She stroked his friendly head.

And it was then that Anahita noticed what lay at her feet, what she had stumbled over the night before. It was a pile of gold coins, huge to her now but exactly the same as the ones Lizard had brought her when she was ill.

They winked in the shadows. Rat saw her looking puzzled. He picked up a coin in his mouth and ran a short way up the tunnel. Lizard picked up another and ran a short way down.

Anahita thought she understood: Rat had brought the coins as far as the nest, Lizard carried them on to her little house. They had been working together to help her.

'Oh, my lovely, kind friends,' she said and hugged them with both arms.

Then all three climbed into the rat's nest and shared the grape.

Mountains of Gold

The morning dew had been burned away. The sun stood above the rooftops. For an hour men had been at their work.

But the nest beneath the city was so dark and comfortable that even though Anahita had just got up, she nearly fell asleep again. Her companions did. With Rat snoring gently on one side and Lizard whistling down his nostrils on the other, she lay wondering:

Where was she?

Where had Rat found the gold?

What on earth was going to happen next?

Who, or what, were her strange new friends? She had never heard of a lizard which helped old ladies, or a rat which brought gifts and wanted to be loved.

And finally what, if anything, could be done to put a stop to Zohak Ali and his reign of terror? If she could find an answer to that, thought Anahita, perhaps she could regain her proper size – even her long-lost youth.

Just the morning before, by chance, as she was making her final purchases for the feast, a fruit seller had passed on a rumour that was circulating in the city. A slave had escaped from the Blue Palace and sought refuge in the Great Mosque. He was young and had many tales to tell of life within the palace walls. If he was to be believed, extraordinary things took place there.

One detail was of particular interest to Anahita. In his study Zohak Ali kept a big red book in which all his spells were written down. It wasn't the first time there had been mention of this book. In fact, it was often a topic of conversation in the city. Had not Anahita and a hundred others seen it with their own eyes on the morning of Zohak Ali's arrival from the desert with his great caravan. What kind of book needed to be carried at his saddle, bound with a strong chain and padlocked? It must be very important. And why did he ensure that none of his slaves could read? Sultan Mushtaq and the other slave owners never gave it a thought, but on his rare visits to the slave market this was the magician's first question. Was it because of the red book? The slave hiding in the Great Mosque said it was.

But Anahita *could* read, although not well. And as she lay puzzling in Rat's cosy nest she realized that if she could gain access to the Blue Palace and find her way to the magician's study, the big book might, just might, provide her with the knowledge she needed. She gave her companions a nudge.

Rat yawned. Lizard woke up.

'I don't know if you can understand me,' Anahita said. 'If you can, do you think we could get into the Blue Palace?'

They looked at her. Bright eyes reflected a sunbeam. Then Lizard scratched his back. Rat snuffled into his fur and licked vigorously.

Two hours later. The maze had been left behind and they were far up a single tunnel. It was a steep climb. Rat led the way, followed by Lizard with Anahita holding on to his tail.

A big space opened up ahead. Rat halted. Anahita tumbled over Lizard. They waited to see if it was safe to continue.

All was silent.

Then somewhere a door shut and there was a sound of footsteps. A light glimmered at the far side of a great cavern. It was high up in the wall beyond some bend. Rat pulled back into the tunnel. They watched.

A lantern appeared. Anahita gasped. It was Zohak Ali. Gripping a rail, he descended a long flight of steps.

They were in the magician's treasure house, the cave within the hill. On all sides lay mountains of gold and

fabulous ornaments. The light from his lantern covered the roof with dancing reflections. He felt in his pocket for Anahita's three coins and tossed them on to the heap from which, unguessed by himself, they had come. He dug in his fingers, letting the gold stream through them like water. Caskets of diamonds and rubies flashed fire. Coronets and tiaras had fallen to the floor; necklaces of opal and pearl trailed from baskets. He put an enamelled mask from the tomb of a Pharaoh to his face and looked through the eyes; trailed a shawl of filigree gold about his shoulders; examined the sacred statues of a god and a demon and cast them contemptuously back on the pile.

Beyond an arch lay a smaller chamber. Within lay something pale. Zohak Ali walked through and Anahita saw a mound of skulls and skeletons. She suppressed a cry. A skull had fallen and bowled across the floor. The magician kicked it back. A skeleton, too, was slithering down. He grasped it by a rib and tossed it up on the heap. The bones made a sharp, cracking, rattling noise. Anahita cringed but Zohak liked the sound. Taking two skulls, he tapped them together and did a little dance. His grotesque shadow leaped on the wall. Anahita prayed that the remains of her father and brother were not in that terrible place.

Zohak Ali had seen all he wanted. His treasure was safe. Taking up the lantern, he crossed to the stone steps and returned the way he had come. The light glimmered into darkness. His door banged shut.

Rat waited, for who could tell what spies and beasts the magician had in his pay or in his power. He had been there many times, but perhaps since his last visit a colony of bats had been installed in the roof, or a venomous snake on the ground. He sniffed the air. Peered this way and that. Looked to the others for reassurance.

As soon as all seemed safe, Rat ventured from the tunnel. Lizard and Anahita followed. Staying close to the wall, they started round the treasure cave. The mountain of coins lay in their path. They tried to climb over but avalanches slid away beneath their feet and filled the cave with a jingle of gold. They fled back to the safety of the tunnel. Rat knocked over a jar. It smashed. Emeralds scattered the floor like marbles. Anahita trod on them and fell. It seemed certain they must be discovered.

But no one came.

With thudding hearts they set off again, circling the hill of coins, and soon were halfway to the magician's steps. Rat halted. A ragged crack ran up the cave wall. He climbed a metre. He could have run all the way to the top. So could Lizard. It was not so easy for Anahita. Not only was she an old lady, she was terrified of heights. Nevertheless, she took a determined breath, reached up in the darkness and began to climb.

It was a long way, several times higher than Anahita when she was her proper size. The rock crumbled; she could not find footholds; her knees shook with fright. But at length, helped by Lizard from behind and Rat, whose tail was her safety line, from in front, she reached the top. Rat leaned out, caught her dress in his teeth, and pulled her over the edge.

As soon as Anahita had recovered they set off again. The tunnel they had entered was more earthy than the one below and criss-crossed by roots. The ends of worms waved from the walls. Rat pounced on a tasty beetle. The tunnel was also much shorter and soon, looking past her companions, she saw daylight ahead, green daylight from the reflection of leaves.

Before they emerged, Rat halted again, eyes, ears, nose and whiskers alert to danger. No alarm signals came from nearby though Anahita heard a deep, coughing, growling sound a short distance away. She did not like it at all.

One at a time the black rat, yellow lizard and tiny old lady emerged into the daylight. The tunnel was a few centimetres above ground level and hidden by a laurel bush. They descended a bank, crept across dry leaves and peeped out from beneath.

Anahita clapped a hand over her mouth. They were in the garden of the Blue Palace.

The Garden
of Statues

The gardens of Sultan Mushtaq were formal, cool
and beautiful. The gardens of the Blue Palace were
different. There was more than a hint of the jungle
about them. Leopards and a pair of tigers lay in the
shade of trees which, though planted only recently,
grew luxuriantly about the walls. The lawns were neat-
ly trimmed — two slaves in tiger-proof suits were on
hands and knees cutting them as the three friends
emerged — but the wilderness threatened. Blossom fell,
seeds scattered, greedy tendrils reached across the
grass. A score of lifesize statues, each on a plinth, were
being engulfed by tropical vines.

Somewhere a voice called out, and then a second
voice, but they were too far off for the words to be dis-
tinguishable.

Rat, Lizard and Anahita crept away from the

safety of the tunnel. Unfortunately the undergrowth which gave them protection also afforded it to a host of terrifying insects and other garden creatures. A spider stood knee-high; beetles like armadillos came scuttling to investigate; an earthworm wrapped around Anahita's leg; a horsefly with enough poison to kill her stone dead settled on her dress. Had it not been for the appetites of Lizard and Rat, Anahita might not have lasted long.

There were bigger enemies too. A tiger spotted them and bounded up to look more closely. There was *no* defence against a Bengal tiger. They scattered: Lizard up the nearest tree; Anahita down among the roots; and Rat — well, Anahita never saw where Rat went.

The hollow where she was crouching turned dark. She looked up and found the tiger's face blocking out the light. He looked puzzled and put out a paw to investigate. A claw as long as herself broke a strand of root. He scraped at the earth. She was enveloped in tiger breath.

Rescue came from an unexpected source. Rosh had been to the house and found it abandoned. Now, circling above the city, he spotted a juicy rat dashing between bushes in a wild garden. Instantly he dived. The air rushed past. He stretched out his talons. At the last second he saw the tiger raking beneath a tree. He swerved aside, startled, and settled on the garden wall.

The tiger ducked and looked up with tawny eyes. The hawk stared back at him, completely unafraid.

The tiger left his prey in the roots of the tree and roared. He bounded at Rosh and sprang up the wall. It was too high. Rosh lowered his head, shouted *Ky-ow! Ky-ow!* and rattled his wings with defiance.

Seeing the way clear, Anahita crawled from her refuge and ran off into deeper shadow.

Rosh spotted her beyond his snarling adversary; saw her clearly with his sharp vision; recognized her. A second time he was startled then returned to taunting the tiger.

Where were the others? Anahita searched. Had it not been for the sun shining through leaves and glimpses of the Blue Palace, she would have been completely lost.

Zohak's garden was different from the Sultan's in a second way. There were nasty things. Through the foliage Anahita spotted a low wall and tiptoed towards it. She climbed on top, hoping to get a better view. It was lucky she did not fall off the far side for below lay a big green pool. Logs were floating among water lilies. She was puzzled until one log suddenly leaped at another, mouth gaping. They were crocodiles.

A hot stony pit in another part of the garden was the home of cobras and other venomous snakes. A bird trap nearby was full of pretty finches and linnets. Judging by the feathers in the pit, they were being caught to feed the snakes. She opened the door with difficulty and watched them all fly away.

Anahita longed to call to her friends but dared not.

She crept on, frightened and alone. And suddenly came upon the most terrible thing she had encountered yet in the magician's garden. If it had not been for the voice she might never have noticed:

'All hail to thee, great Zohak Ali, Lord of Samarkand.'

Anahita jumped out of her skin. It was a man's voice, close beside her. She ran to hide beneath an over-hanging weed. No foot stamped upon her. No giant hand appeared to pluck her out. All was silent. She caught her breath; slowly her heart stopped thudding. And it was only then, thinking back, that she realized she knew the voice – or thought she did. It must be some trick. She peeped out. Before her lay a lawn; behind stood the rampant jungle. Apart from a beetle with very nasty-looking pincers, the only living thing in sight was an armour-clad gardener cutting the grass.

Where had the voice come from? She emerged, feeling very exposed, and crept towards the plinth of a nearby statue.

'All hail to thee, immortal Zohak, Master of the Mysteries.'

Anahita suppressed a scream. She covered her head. But again nothing happened. And she *did* recognize the voice. It was her father. She was sure of it. But where was he? And why was he chanting these strange praises? She stared around wildly. No one was there. She looked behind the plinth, behind tree trunks, in bushes, through a thicket of bamboo. Nothing but a scorpion and more of those scary insects. She returned to her original spot.

'All hail to thee, majestic Zohak, creator and destroyer.'

A third time Anahita jumped. It was so unexpected. But this time she realized the voice had come from overhead. She looked up. There was nothing above her but the blue sky, a few high branches and the sun-dappled statue. Anahita shaded her eyes to look more closely — and froze with horror. It was a statue of her father. More than a statue, in fact, so lifelike that if it had not been made of stone she would have believed her father himself was standing there. Birds had dirtied the head. Ivy grew past its waist.

But where had the voice come from? 'Father?' she said. 'Father?'

There was no reply. She walked all round, clambering through the grass.

'All hail to thee, great Zohak Ali, Lord of Samarkand.'

The statue was speaking, the stone lips moved. The blind stone eyes stared ahead. She stood back to see better then came close again.

'All hail to thee, immortal Zohak, Master of the Mysteries.'

Every time she approached, the statue repeated the mantras: 'All hail to thee . . . All hail to thee . . .' Was this really her father, she wondered, turned to stone?

Or was her father somewhere else, locked up or dead, and this was merely a likeness, like the statues of Alexander and Timur in the market square? Tiny Anahita wept and pressed her cheek against an ivy-free corner of the plinth.

A cheetah approached and she had to move on.

There were many statues, several surrounding the lawns, others barely visible through the vegetation. Was one of them, she wondered, a statue of her missing brother? Or Prince Sohrab? If her father was there, it seemed possible.

She ducked behind the edge of the lawn so that the gardener would not spot her, and ran to the next statue. It was a man she did not recognize.

'All hail to thee, majestic Zohak,' the statue chanted as she came too close, 'creator and destroyer.'

The gardener did not even look up. He had heard it a thousand times. Birds, frogs, set them off.

Anahita hurried on. She knew the face of the next statue. It was a boy she sometimes saw in the market.

She was so small that even a fallen blossom was an obstacle, and it took minutes to scramble from one statue to the next. It was dangerous, too, and she found a twig with a long thorn to repel persistent beetles. Anxiously, as she approached each statue, she examined its stone clothes and looked up into its stone face. None was of Farraj or Prince Sohrab.

She visited eight, standing back to avoid their calling out, and recognized only one more, a kindly muezzin who had called the faithful to prayer from the tower of the Great Mosque.

There were others but the distances were too great and it was time to find Lizard and Rat, wherever they were. Long past time, they would think she had been eaten by the tiger! As she returned along the border of the lawn a flock of little birds descended through the canopy of leaves. Some landed on the heads of the statues. 'All hail to thee,' the statues cried and some birds flew off but most remained. 'All hail to thee, great Zohak Ali.' The birds twitched their tails and wiped their beaks on the stone hair and turbans.

A flash of yellow in the undergrowth and Lizard was at her side. He led the way and Anahita was reunited with Rat in a vine thicket halfway up the garden wall. She was relieved to be back with her friends. What their adventures had been during the past hour she had no idea.

Rat examined a sore patch on his tail. Anahita hoped she had not caused it during their ascent of the cave wall. Then she remembered her mother throwing a spoon at the rat by her fireplace. That had hit the creature on the tail and hurt it because it had squeaked. Could they be the same rat? Could it have been Rat in her mother's living room? She watched him and he looked up then went on snuffling and licking. There was no way of knowing.

For a while they rested then Lizard, munching on a

dragonfly, wriggled up through twigs to the top of the wall. Rat and Anahita followed.

Where was Rosh? All three looked over their shoulders. He was not to be seen, the sky was empty. Feeling very visible, they set off along the wall towards the Blue Palace.

If the garden had not grown so magically fast, it would have been inviting disaster. But now the wall was overhung by branches and fronds of bamboo. For metres at a time they had to scramble through thorns and ivy leaves. Whatever danger they faced on top of the wall, it was less than the danger down in the garden.

Anahita wondered why the cheetahs and panthers did not escape. It would have been so easy for them to climb out. Zohak Ali must have put a spell on them, she thought, or perhaps they were so well fed they didn't want to leave the garden. Was there any connection, she shivered, between the big cats and the pile of skeletons in the treasure room? Could one of them be Farraj? A leopard coughed a warning and stretched up towards her. Anahita hurried after her companions.

The Blue Palace rose before them. A wall like a stone trellis, covered with hibiscus, separated the garden from an inner courtyard. Swinging and wriggling from gap to gap, they descended.

The Magician's Study

The courtyard, in contrast to the rampant garden, was elegant and spacious.

A magnificent fountain stood in the middle. Water spouted from the mouths of demons and splashed over the heads of gods and maidens. Ornamental fish swam in the surrounding pool. Water birds with dagger beaks dived in and beat the fish to death on the stonework. A seat had been placed in the shade of an orange tree. Zohak Ali found it relaxing to sit by the fountain with his hookah and watch the slaughter.

He was reclining there, hidden from sight, as the three companions reached the ground and started round the courtyard behind twenty-metre palms that lined the outer wall. Together they dashed from trunk to trunk. It was Rat who smelled the tobacco smoke and Anahita who spotted it drifting above the branches. By this time they were halfway to a blue-green arch that led into the palace.

Anahita looked to right and left. The open court-yard was empty. No one looked from the palace windows. Leaving Rat and Lizard, she made a dash to the shelter of the tree. Her feet made a tiny slap on the watered stones but if Zohak Ali heard it he paid no attention. She regained her breath and crept through the trailing branches.

Before her lay the fountain and closer at hand, bare-ly three metres away, the figure of Zohak Ali. His back was towards her. To his left sat a beautiful black girl with a dulcimer on her knees. On a table to his right sat the bubbling hookah, its long tube snaking to his lips. Blue smoke rose into the orange leaves.

'Music.' He gestured with a languid hand and the slave girl began to play.

He paid her no attention, his eyes stayed downwards towards his knees. Anahita was intrigued. What was he looking at? Not the fountain or the birds. She slipped back through the branches and moved to one side where she could see more clearly. Cautiously she peered round the tree trunk. Anahita caught her breath. The red book she was seeking rested in the magician's lap. He turned the page with a hand heavy with rings. His hooded eyes moved down the lines of writing. Taking the hookah from his lips, he smiled then threw back his head and laughed softly.

The slave girl appeared relieved to find her master in

such a good mood. He looked at her. 'You play very sweetly.'

Anahita crept away and hurried back to her companions. 'We've *got* to get inside the palace,' she told them. 'Find the study and hide. He's got the book with him.'

She had told them her plan though whether they had understood anything it was hard to say. At that moment they were more agitated by her reckless dash across open ground. Rat pushed her crossly with his nose. Anahita sat down with a bump.

Taking care not to rustle any fallen leaves, they continued round the courtyard and came to the palace entrance. Though not the main entrance, it was a magnificent arch decorated with mosaic, marble and beaten gold. Lizard ran ahead to see if the way was clear.

It was the hottest part of the day. Samarkand baked in the afternoon sun but within the hilltop palace the air was cool and refreshing. They kept close to the wall and hid behind a man-sized urn. Three heads peeped out. They were in a tremendous entrance hall. High walls rose on every side, walls split by doors, pillars, balconies, a great staircase, windows spilling shafts of light, friezes depicting the triumphs of Zohak Ali. Beyond a distant window Anahita saw a rose garden. This could, she thought for the hundredth time, have been her home.

A barefoot slave crossed the floor. In his hands was

a tank teeming with fish to replenish the fountain. He passed out into the sunlight.

They ran on, from urn to pillar and tumbling fern. A hunting dog slept at the foot of the stairs. They slipped through a curtain and found themselves in a richly-furnished drawing room. A second room, with a long table and hunting trophies, was for feasting; a third for music and entertainment. Zohak Ali, it was said, liked dancing girls.

Chamber followed chamber. A scent of herbs and baking meats drifted down a long corridor. Where was the study? Anahita was lost.

Swift footsteps approached. They dodged through the nearest doorway and found themselves in a bathing room. Cool mosaics of an underwater scene covered the walls. Rattan chests and towels and jars of perfumed oil stood near a sunken bath big enough to swim in. They hid. The footsteps came closer. Anahita peeped towards the door. Zohak Ali strode past. Beneath his arm was the red leather book of spells. His footsteps receded. She raced across the tiled floor and looked after him. The corner of his cloak swished from sight.

What should they do?

Lizard emerged. Then Rat. They joined her at the door.

And they were still there, in open view, when Zohak Ali returned. His footsteps were softer, perhaps he had changed his shoes. At the last moment Rat heard him and dashed for cover. The others followed. Had the great magician glanced into his bathing room as he passed, he would have seen a yellow lizard and a black rat streaking across the floor with a tiny ragged lady in pursuit. But he did not look into his bathing room, his thoughts were elsewhere, and by the time Anahita reached her hiding place he was ten metres down the corridor.

As soon as the coast was clear they resumed their search of the palace. Anahita rounded the corner where she had seen Zohak Ali disappear with the book. A parrot shrieked: 'Gaaak! Master! Master!' A house-cheetah crossed ahead of them. Death seemed on every side.

By good luck and Rat's sixth sense they managed to avoid discovery and at length came to a room with a sturdy wooden door. It was ajar. Anahita peeped through. Her heart leaped. It was the magician's study. She beckoned the others and ventured inside.

It was a big room with windows in two walls. One faced the jungle garden, the other high across Samarkand to the palace of Sultan Mushtaq. Unlike the other rooms in the Blue Palace, this was a work room. Half, they saw, was the magician's library with a wall of books, an easy chair and rich rugs on the floor. The other half was his laboratory. Anahita gazed at the tables spread with experiments, the magical apparatus, the astrolabes, zodiacs, jars and phials, charts, bones, bottles, maps, globes, symbols, claws, brains, teeth, powders, pendulums, scarabs, philtres, herbs, wax figures, anatomical diagrams, crucibles, fetishes, pestles and mortars, animal skulls, spectacles, hares' feet and microscopes. The air smelled of smoke and something exotic.

In the middle of the room stood the magician's ornate desk. From floor level the objects that lay upon it were hidden but just above the edge Anahita saw the corner of a thick red book. Her hopes surged.

Lizard kept watch at the gap in the door while Rat and Anahita ran across the room. They did not know about the magic alarm, the invisible rings which circled the desk to protect the book from prying eyes. But Zohak Ali had never imagined intruders less than fifteen centimetres tall and they passed beneath like birds under a gate. By good fortune he had thrown a cloak over the back of his chair. They climbed up. Rat jumped from the arm to the desk and helped Anahita across.

The book she was seeking lay before her with a quill pen at its side. All around stood pots of ink and notes and extinguished candles and an empty wineglass and a scatter of debris. The lettering on the cover was so big and faded it was hard to read. Anahita climbed on top and walked along each word. Letter by letter she spelled out the title:

'S-O-R-C-E-R-Y A-N-D S-P-E-L-L-S. This is it!' she cried to Rat. 'His book of spells! This is what I was looking for.'

Rat regarded her with bright button eyes.

She clambered down to the desk and pushed at the leather cover. It was so big and heavy that little Anahita could hardly move it let alone open it. 'Come on, Rat.' She struggled. 'Give me a hand.'

He was much stronger and managed to wedge a shoulder underneath the corner but was so clumsy that he could do no more. The cover opened a few centimetres and then fell shut. He tried again. And again.

But although Rat was no good at opening books, he was very good at gnawing. Running to the far side of the volume, he began to nibble down the spine. Fragments of cardboard, dry glue and sun-faded leather littered the desk top.

It took a long time. Anahita was terrified they would be discovered. But no one came. Perhaps, she thought, slaves were forbidden to enter the study; perhaps they were resting in the heat of the day.

At last the spine was nibbled through. They tugged the cover aside. It fell and hit the floor with a heavy thump. They looked towards the door. Lizard maintained his vigil. All was quiet.

Anahita began to turn the pages, thick yellowed pages covered with Zohak Ali's bold handwriting. Each one was an effort. She lifted the corner, crawled inside the book, stood up and heaved the page over. Rat watched her and understood. They developed a routine. Anahita lifted the corner, Rat ran inside, stood up on his hind legs and scrabbled at the page with his claws.

Spell followed spell. She read the titles: *Stars, Beetles, Whirlwinds, Fire, Auguries, Poisons, Vanishing, Blood, Stone, Vegetation, Crystal Gazing, Immobility,* more than she could have dreamed of. But at last, as Rat, staggering with effort, prepared to throw over page one hundred and fifty-seven, Anahita cried, 'Stop!'

There it was: *Shrivelling and Shrinking.* She crawled up on to the book. Like every other spell, at the end there was a footnote: *To Reverse.* Anahita read it carefully, then read it again and jumped down.

'Dust,' she said. 'We need dust, green and silver, sprackling.'

She stared around. What *sprackling* meant she had no idea.

The pots of dust stood on a high shelf on the laboratory wall. Her heart fell, there was *no* way she could climb up to that. And even if she could, she would be unable to screw off the top. She tried to read the labels but they were too far away.

Lizard watched them from the door. Anahita had an idea. She might not be able to climb the wall but Lizard could. And even if he couldn't read, he could push down the jars.

Followed by Rat, she slid down the cloak and ran back across the floor. Rat gave a little hop of excitement and missed the magic ring by a whisker. Earnestly Anahita explained her plan to Lizard and pointed up. He seemed to understand. But the laboratory floor was tiled. When the jars fell they would smash, servants might hear. All three strained against the door. It shut with a click. Then Lizard, bright-eyed and yellow as a sunflower, ran up the wall to the shelf.

Rat and the tiny old lady stood back. Lizard pushed with all his might. The first jar slid to the edge, toppled and hit the floor like a bomb. The container shattered. An explosion of red dust filled the air. Rat sneezed and turned pink. He sneezed again and turned blue. He returned to normal. Anahita ran forward and read the label, just to be sure.

She looked up. Some of the labels were turned towards the wall. A second jar hurtled towards her. She jumped aside. A yellow explosion. She was covered from head to foot. It had no effect. She brushed herself clean.

Black dust!

Orange!

Silvery green!

'Stop! Stop!' She ran forward again. The label stuck to a fragment of pot. She heaved it from beneath the powder and blew it clean.

Dust, read Anahita. *Green and Silver: Sprackling.*

'This is it!' she cried.

Lizard looked down from his high shelf.

'We've got it,' Anahita called up. 'Oh, thank you, lovely, lovely Lizard. You can come down now.'

Rat was still sneezing but inhaling all those magic dusts seemed to have done him little harm. Once he turned lilac and twice his fur stood straight out on end like a bottle brush, but mostly he was his handsome self.

Anahita took a fat pinch of the green and silver powder and ran to the window that overlooked the jungle garden. It was a few centimetres open for ventilation. The sun streamed in. It was the most dust-free part of the room.

Rat and Lizard stood back and watched.

She shut her eyes and made a wish. Then, spinning three times anticlockwise, she cried the words she had learned from the book: 'Fig! Fennel! Frangipani!' and threw the dust over her head.

The next instant she knew what *sprackling* meant for all around her the air was sparkling and crackling like a firework. For a second Anahita felt as if her skin was going to burst like an over-ripe plum. Her eyes popped, the floor shot away beneath her. All at once she was her proper size again.

She felt huge, colossal, big as an elephant. Rat and Lizard, who had been bigger than she was, were suddenly little, right down by her shoes. And startled. She bent down to reassure them and put out a hand. It did not occur to her at first that her hand was old, she was so used to seeing it. One side of the window was shaded by leaves. She stepped close to see her reflection. The same wrinkled face with a big nose that she had lived with for so long gazed back at her. She bared her broken teeth.

But little by little, as Anahita stood there, a second

change was taking place. The first spell, years old, was also reversing, only slowly, as if it were hard-set, or the magic had spent most of its energy returning her to her proper size. Her fingertips began to prickle like pins and needles. She looked down, fearing some new ageing horror, but the very opposite was happening: her fingernails, her fingers, the backs of her hands were losing their clawed, reptilian appearance. The change spread up her arms. Her toes, too, began to tingle. Her stick-like legs filled out. Her back straightened. The wild grey hair that straggled across her face turned black again. Her teeth were white and even. She touched her cheek, it was young.

Shaken by sobs, Anahita regarded herself in the window. She hardly recognized the girl who stood there. Not only was she two years older, her face was dirty, her clothes even dirtier and hanging in rags – not a girl's clothes at all, the clothes of a rich old woman.

Down by her feet, Lizard and Rat were hopping and jumping, running in circles, setting their paws against her ankles and looking up. They too wanted something from the book of spells but there was no time. From a short way off came a noise of voices, shouting, running footsteps.

As Zohak Ali reclined by the fountain he had felt the magic in the air. There had been no alarm, no sign of intruders, but the sprackling made his skin tingle. He sprang to his feet. 'Quiet!' he snarled at the girl with a dulcimer and lifted his face as if scenting the breeze.

Where had it come from? The only possibility was his study. He roused the palace.

Anahita stared around in panic. There was a big iron key in the door. She locked it and ran to the window facing the jungle garden. A leopard lay outside. It yawned, showing needle-sharp teeth. She looked from the second window. Beneath was a long drop down the palace wall. They were trapped. Then her eyes fell on the fireplace. She pushed aside the hummingbird screen and peered up the chimney. It was open to the sky.

The first slaves reached the door. Fists thudded on the panels.

Anahita scooped up Lizard and Rat and popped them into her pockets. The little pile of green and silver dust lay a few paces away. She tumbled a handful over Rat's head. The big book of spells lay on the desk. As she went to take it she ran straight through the invisible rings. It was potent magic. Instantly the palace was a chaos of crashing bells. She snatched the book up. How could she carry it? Zohak Ali's robe trailed over the chair. She pulled out the thick silk cord, slotted it between the pages, tied a knot and hung the damaged book over her shoulder.

Then, slipping past the fire-screen, she reached up the chimney and began to climb.

Flight from the Blue Palace

High overhead throughout the Blue Palace the great bells crashed and clashed and swung. The spell had been too strong. Chandeliers shivered, ornaments danced on the shelves. It was impossible to think because of the noise.

'Stop!' Zohak Ali clapped hands over his ears. 'Stop it! Stop it!'

But no one knew how to stop it.

He cast a reversing spell but in the madness of the moment got it wrong. The noise intensified. Mirrors cracked, windows exploded, the camera obscura began to break apart. He cast a second spell. Enormous spider webs snatched the bells in mid peal.

The palace fell silent — silent except for the cries of deafened slaves. Those not near enough to hear the magician's shouts had heard the alarm bells. Leaving their labours in courtyard and kitchen, they converged on the study. Barefooted and bare-chested, they clustered by the door.

'Be quiet! Stop your whining!' Zohak Ali flung them aside and seized the handle, a bronze handle in the shape of a dragon's head. He turned it. The door was locked. In a fury he shook it and turned to the slave who stood nearest. 'Set your hand on the lock.'

He was an African slave in yellow pantaloons. 'But, Master—'

'Set your hand on the lock!' the magician repeated. 'Give me the other.'

The frightened man did so. A flicker of lightning ran through him like blue fire and the door burst open. The slave screamed, nursing his broken hand. They ran past him into the room.

Sunbeams cut a swathe through the floating dust. They saw the broken pots, the fallen robe, the cover of the book of spells.

The magician gave a loud cry: 'My book! Oh, my book!' He turned in terrible anger. 'Whoever did this, seek him out. Find him. Bring him to me!'

They looked from the garden window. The leopard, disturbed by the commotion, had vanished into the bushes.

'Go on! After him!' Zohak Ali drove them forward.

'But, my Lord, the tigers!'

'The panthers!'

'The crocodiles!'

'After him! Go on! You want me to turn you into sheep? You want maggots to eat out your eyes?'

He meant it. The first terrified slave threw wide the window and jumped down into the garden. The shrubbery swallowed him up. Three more followed.

A short way off there was a roar and a shriek. The last man out tried to climb back in. Zohak Ali beat him from the window and pulled it shut. His terror-stricken face stared through the glass.

The remaining slaves fled.

The magician picked up the cover of his book, the repository of his power, his lifetime's study. He stared from the second window. Beneath him lay Samarkand. The city would pay for this!

As he turned away he saw that his beautiful fire-screen had been moved. He put out a hand to straighten it. A scatter of soot lay in the hearth. He looked more closely. The intruder hadn't escaped through the window at all.

'The chimney! The chimney, you fools! He's up on the roof!'

He spun round. The study was deserted. He ran from the room, robes flying. 'The roof!' His voice faded along the corridors. 'Up on the roof! Where are you? Hurry! Hurry!'

Out in the garden there was another bloodcurdling scream.

The roofs of the Blue Palace were many and flat. Anahita emerged from the chimney and jumped down.

She looked like the dirtiest kind of vagabond: her clothes were in shreds, from head to heel she was streaked with earth from the tunnel, cobwebs from the garden, dust from the study and soot from the chimney.

She ran to the edge and looked down. Beneath her lay the courtyard, the garden, a long drop down the palace wall. There seemed no escape that way. A trapdoor gave access to the roof from within the palace. She tugged the ringbolt. It was locked from the inside. Close by, a flight of steps led from her roof to the very topmost roof of the palace. Nothing in the whole of Samarkand stood higher except the magician's tower.

She ran up. The roof was surrounded by a low parapet. Anahita peeped over. The drop was fearsome but there was nowhere else to go. How could she get down? Her eyes flew to the flagpole. Zohak Ali's standard, the black phoenix, hung slack in the sun. The excess rope was coiled at the bottom. Quickly she lowered the flag and untied it. The rope slid through the top pulley and fell at her feet. She tied an end round the pole and threw the rest over the parapet. It just reached the hillside far below. She was terrified, the height made her dizzy. But if she stayed, Anahita realized, her fate would be even worse than if she fell. And what about poor Rat and Lizard? She clambered over the parapet. Hand over hand she began to lower herself to the ground.

By the time Zohak Ali had rounded up his slaves and

reached the roof she was almost to the bottom. He saw the rope and ran to the parapet.

It wasn't possible. 'You again! When I catch hold of you this time I'll—'

One of the slaves had been sweeping sand in a court-yard. Zohak seized his broom and flung it down. It hit Anahita on the arm. She lost her grip and fell the last metre. The hillside was steep. Unable to stop herself, she bowled on head over heels into thick bushes.

'Get after her!' Zohak Ali beat his slaves about the shoulders. 'My book! I must have my book! Go on! Down the rope!' He grabbed one by the hair and drove him over the parapet. Another followed.

But he had reckoned without Rosh. Tired of annoy-ing the tiger, Rosh had flown up to the tower. Sitting on a familiar ledge, he spent a long time grooming. Now, feathers in order, he saw and somehow, in the recesses of his hawk brain, recognized Anahita as she ran from roof to roof and descended the rope. These men were pursuing her. Screaming his harsh *Ky-ow! Ky-ow!* he launched himself from the ledge. The poor slaves, hanging in space, found themselves under attack by a feathered demon. His wings buffeted their faces, his talons and beak ripped their backs. They struck out blindly but Rosh was too swift. First one, then the other fell to the rocky hillside and bounced on down into the bushes where Anahita was hiding. One even crashed into her but they were much too shaken and sore to take any notice of the girl they were pursuing.

Zohak Ali shouted and shook his fist. This attracted Rosh's attention. He did not like this noisy man who leaned over the parapet. He did, however, like the flashing egg in his turban. In a sudden switch of direction, he fastened his talons round the Bangalore diamond and wrenched the turban from the magician's head.

It came unravelled. Metre after metre of fine black silk trailed in the air as Rosh flew away, high into the blue beyond the city.

While Zohak Ali cursed, a slave who was too frightened to descend the rope untied it from the flagpole and threw it over.

The magician's hair hung past his shoulders. In a fury he struck the man dead. There was no other way down. 'Round by the gate,' he cried. 'Bring her to me. Hurry! Hurry!'

'But, my Lord,' exclaimed a slave with one eye. 'She is in the city.'

'What?' Zohak Ali stared at the man.

'We cannot leave the palace. Your magic makes it impossible.'

'I renounce the spell.' The great magician threw back his head to face the sky. He crossed his wrists, spread his fingers and flung his arms wide as if in ecstasy. 'Hosharak! Zagriel!' he cried.

The slaves drew back, awaiting some sign: some flash, or rumbling voice, or shaking of the earth. Nothing occurred.

* *. * .*.* .* * *. 121 * * * .* .* . *.* .

'The way is clear. Now go! Go!' he told them. 'Search the hillsides, search the streets. Find her! Bring me my book!'

The dead slave lay at his feet. He ran at them. With shouts they fled: tumbling from roof to roof, down through the trapdoor, along the corridors and out into the baking courtyards.

The spell which had kept a hundred slaves imprisoned in the Blue Palace was broken. He had given them permission to leave. It was enough. What did they care about the girl or a book they could not read? Reaching the gate they scattered like bright sparrows into the lanes and hidden corners of the city never to return.

Zohak Ali, meanwhile, climbed to the top of the tower from where he could observe everything. He had seen Rosh before, watched the big mountain hawk fly to the house of the rich old lady who had tried to kill him. He had seen Anahita, young again, fall from the rope. He had seen his precious, irreplaceable book hanging from her shoulder. Now he watched his slaves run off into the city. His life, his plans, were descending into chaos. All because of that wretched girl. 'My book!' he roared. 'Come back!' If the slaves heard, they did not respond. He let them go, it didn't matter. Slaves were ten a penny.

More important, infinitely more important, was the girl on the hillside. He watched her scramble down through the bushes, too far off for his magic to work. Even dirty and dishevelled, how graceful she was. How he hated her! She vanished among workyards and shabby stables. Where would she go, to her mother's or back to the house near the pigsties?

She emerged into the narrow street. People stared as she ran past them in her ragged finery, the heavy book clasped in her arms. Zohak Ali watched. She seemed to be heading for the house by the pigsties. She must not know it had been ransacked.

But Anahita was not running anywhere. She was running away, that was all, running as fast and as far from the terrors of the Blue Palace as her legs would carry her.

Candles
and Salt

Anahita looked back over her shoulder as she ran.
Zohak Ali, hands braced on the parapet, stood watching from his high tower. She dodged into the doorway
of a mosque to catch her breath.

Lizard and Rat, bruised and shaken, looked from her
pockets. Rat sneezed and shook the dust from his
head.

'I'm so sorry.' Anahita stroked them with her finger.
'Not much further.'

But not much further to where? Until what? There
was nothing at the pig house. Her old home seemed
the only possibility. Zohak Ali would search for her in
both places but she had a good start. At least she could
get her mother out of danger.

She peeped back at the Blue Palace. The tower was
deserted. He was after her already. She emerged from

the mosque and ran on, through the market and down the narrow alleys to her mother's house.

The door was open. Anahita hurried through the abandoned workshop and burst into the living room.

Fatima screamed with fright. 'What do you want? Who are you? Get out! Get out! There's nothing here to steal. I'm just a poor old woman.' Then she looked more closely and recognized her daughter. 'Anahita!' She screamed again and hugged the dirty, ragged girl to her bosom as if she would never let go.

Thanks to Anahita's gold coins, the room was furnished and respectable again. There was a chair with cushions, a lamp, a dish of fruit. But there was no time to rest or explain. Anahita pushed her mother away and slung the tattered book from her shoulder.

Fatima saw Lizard and Rat peeping from Anahita's pockets. A third time she screamed and backed away.

'Mother, hush!' Anahita locked the door and set Rat and Lizard on a shelf from where they could see what took place.

'Dirty, smelly . . . In my nice clean—!' Fatima seized the cooking pot and would have killed Rat there and then if Anahita had not stopped her.

'No!' She propelled her mother back into her chair. 'I'll explain later. We haven't got much time.'

She set the book on the table and skimmed through the yellowed pages. It didn't take long to find what she was seeking: *Shape-Shifting: Transformation.* There were entries for turning people into animals, insects, trees, stone, and for the magician himself to assume a dozen different forms. Tearing the page in her haste, Anahita found *To Reverse* at the foot of the animal spell and followed the lines of writing with her finger:

'Five fires,
Salt on tongue,
Once, twice, three times turn;
Eyes shut,
Fan the flame,
He who'd be himself again.

Or she, I suppose,' Anahita said. But what did it mean? Luckily there was a brief explanation. She read it carefully, brows knotted, terrified she would need more than the silver-green dust in her pocket. She did, but they were things to be found in any house. For this spell, or counter-spell, the magic dust was of no use at all. Nor were any words required.

'Candles,' she said to her mother. 'And salt. Are they still in the cupboard?'

Fatima had no idea what was happening. She nodded.

Anahita ran across and found a bundle of cheap candles from the market and a jar of crushed salt. Quickly she carried them to the table and lit one. Dripping the wax, she set up five in a ring and lit the remainder. The cones of flame burned brightly as she tipped a little spoonful of salt on to the edge of the table and cleared everything else out of the way.

'Dear Lizard.' She lifted him from the shelf, kissed him lightly and set him in the middle of the table. 'I can't promise it'll work but if it doesn't we'll try again later.'

Lizard blinked his bright, black eyes.

'Are you ready?'

He munched an invisible fly, the closest he could come to talking.

'I'm afraid this is going to taste horrible,' Anahita said. 'Open your mouth.'

He did so and she placed a tiny pinch of salt on his tongue.

'Now, turn three times.'

Lizard chased his tail.

She stopped him with a finger. 'No, the other way.'

Obediently Lizard danced round anticlockwise.

'Face the candles.'

He did as she told him.

'Now, close your eyes and blow the salt into the flames.'

Eyes tight shut, Lizard puffed out his chest and *blew*.

As the salt hit the flames they burned green and blue, flickered for a moment, then blazed up in a flash that filled the room.

Anahita was dazzled. Fatima cried aloud. There was a smell of sulphur and roses. It was a wonder.

But in the heart of the blinding flash a greater wonder had taken place. One second Lizard stood on the

table, yellow and alert, the next he had gone and Prince Sohrab stood in his place.

Anahita and her mother stared.

Sohrab jumped to the floor.

They salaamed deeply.

He raised them up. 'No! No, this is Lizard. It is I who show respect to you.' He took Anahita's hand. 'Brave lady, I owe you my life.'

Rat squeaked for attention.

'Indeed, yes,' said Sohrab. 'Remember Rat. We must be quick.'

Fatima stepped back in disgust as Anahita picked him up. Gently she blew the coloured dusts and other debris out of his fur. 'Darling Rat.' She kissed him too and set him in the middle of the table.

He wiped his whiskers, had a quick scratch and opened his mouth. Rat was clever, after a single demonstration he knew exactly what to do. The second the salt was on his tongue, he spun three times, shut his eyes and blew it over the candle flames. His fur stood on end. A second time a blinding blue flash filled the room. When they could see again Rat was gone and Farraj stood in the middle of his mother's table. But Farraj was taller and bigger-boned than Sohrab and the table was shaky. With a crash it collapsed beneath him.

He stared at his white-haired mother.

Fatima ran through the splinters and flung her arms round the neck of her handsome son.

Anahita was surrounded by the people she loved best

in the world. Only her father was missing. Dimly she was aware of a tiny noise out in the shop. Heat made the boards creak.

Fatima took no notice. She turned to her daughter. 'What are these rags you are wearing? And your face is dirty. Prince Sohrab in our house and you look like a street urchin.'

There was no time, but to do as she said would be quicker than arguing with her mother. Anahita splashed her face and ran to her room. A few clothes remained. Hastily she changed and brushed her hair. Looking more like the girl she had been, she ran back to the living room. 'There, now will you—'

'Sshhh!' Sohrab put a finger to his lips and crossed to the door.

Everyone froze.

'There's somebody in the shop.' He mouthed the words.

Farraj's dark eyes widened. 'Zohak Ali!'

'Quick!' Sohrab said to Anahita. 'Is there a back door?'

She shook her head.

'Then out the window.' He threw it wide.

Anahita grabbed up the book of spells.

'No.' Farraj thrust it at his mother. 'Hide it.'

'What is it?'

He told her.

Fatima threw up her hands. 'Don't give it to me!'

'Mother, you've got to. Anahita risked her life.' He pushed the book into her hands.

'Where?' Her eyes flew about the room.

'I don't know. Think!'

There was a knock at the door.

Fatima gave a diminutive shriek and fled into the further room. Clutching the book to her chest, she jumped into bed and pulled the cover to her eyes.

Farraj laughed. 'Even Zohak Ali won't think of looking there.'

Sohrab was anxious for Anahita. 'Go on, hurry. Your mother's safe. Out the window.'

The knock was repeated.

She was on the sill when the person outside called, 'Who's in there?'

She froze. It was her father's voice, the second time she had heard it that day.

'Somebody open the door.'

'Who is it?' called Sohrab.

'Kashgar,' came the answer. 'Kashgar al Kharif. Who else? This is my house.'

'Father?' Anahita slid back into the room.

'Is that you, daughter?'

Sohrab was uneasy. 'Be careful.'

But Farraj jumped out of the window and ran round to the front of the shop. He peeped inside. A familiar figure stood by the inner door.

'Father!' He ran to embrace him. 'Open the door,'

he called to the three inside. 'It's my father. He's come home.'

Sohrab turned the key and threw the door wide.

Anahita stared. She could not believe it. There stood her beloved father, just as she had seen him in the magician's garden. But this was no statue. She saw his whiskery chin, his greying hair. He smiled a sad smile. She ran across the room.

'Oh, Father! Father, you've come back to us!'

She threw herself into his arms.

Whirlwind

Fatima heard the commotion. She sat up in bed. 'Kashgar! Is that you?'

'Yes, it's me.' His voice drifted through. 'Home at last, my darling.'

She jumped to the floor – then stopped. 'What did you say?'

'I said yes, darling. I'm home.'

It was Kashgar's voice, they were a loving family, but he never called her *darling*. She tiptoed to the door. The man was speaking to Sohrab. He looked like Kashgar. How could he not be Kashgar, her husband of twenty years? Yet Kashgar was warm-hearted while this man – she almost felt the cold. Fatima backed away.

Anahita also drew back. Yes, this was her father but something was wrong. He smelled different – not dirty, just different; his hug had no more love than the clutch of a scarecrow; he did not lay his cheek on her head and call her 'my Heeta'.

Farraj ran to his mother's door. She was getting back into bed.

'Mother?'

'That man is not your father.' She was frightened. 'Who is he? What is happening?'

He stared at her.

She spoke in a whisper. 'He looks like him, I know. But it's not my Kashgar.'

Farraj said, 'You've still got the book?'

She hugged it to her stomach.

He turned back into the living room.

The man who looked like his father saw the expression on their faces. Suddenly he laughed, laughed like a devil with a red mouth and slanting eyes. He flung his arms above his head. There was a black flash and an explosion that threw Sohrab, Anahita and Farraj clear across the room. In the adjoining room Fatima screamed and pulled the bed-cover over her head.

The smoke cleared. Zohak Ali had returned to his proper form. His hair hung loose. There stood the girl who had wreaked such havoc in his life. There stood her interfering brother and that wretched Prince Sohrab. But *where* was his precious, irreplaceable book? He strode through the house, pulled open cupboards, threw over cushions.

'Don't hit me, sir. Don't hit me!' Fatima cowered on her pillow. 'I'm a sick old woman.'

'If you don't stop your whining, you'll be a sick old toad!' Zohak gazed at her contemptuously. 'Where's my book?'

She pulled the bedspread to her nose.

'Where is it?' He strode back into the front room. 'My book, I know you've got it. It's here, isn't it.'

The boys were silent.

'No.' Anahita lifted her chin. 'I threw it into the pigsties. I saw them start to eat it. They'll have finished it by this time. It's gone.'

'You're lying.' He gripped her arm. 'Tell me, or I'll clad your brother and that primrose prince in white-hot suits of armour. This time they'll die!'

She hesitated.

Zohak Ali meant what he threatened. He turned to face Sohrab and Farraj. His eyes blazed. He pointed at them, two fingers spread like a serpent's tongue:

'God of venom,
Fire and flame,
Blood boil
In every—'

Sohrab and Farraj sprang at him. They were not going to stand like hypnotized rabbits waiting to be bewitched all over again. Anahita hit him from behind with a water-jar. Stunned and astonished, the great magician fell to the floor.

They did not linger. Who could tell what power Zohak Ali might possess even if he were tied up and gagged? Pausing only to throw the broken table on top of him, they ran from the house.

A small crowd had gathered. People had heard the explosion and raised voices. Word was spreading that Anahita had returned. Now the missing Prince Sohrab, in his white robes and golden turban, came running from the shoemaker's shop.

There was a cry of astonishment.

'Follow me.' Sohrab was a leader. 'To the market square.'

He pushed through the crowd. In a flood they followed him along the alley. It emptied.

But Anahita and Farraj were anxious for their mother. How could they help her? Powerless against Zohak Ali's magic, they hid opposite the shop and watched — and waited.

Close to the wall of the Great Mosque which stood alongside the square, Sohrab sprang up on to an empty fruit cart. The people gathered before him:

'My friends,' Sohrab cried. 'The hour has come. It is time to put a stop to the wickedness that rules our lives. You have suffered too long. We have all suffered too long. The evil Zohak Ali has taken your children, stolen your money, robbed you of your dignity as free men and women. The city is on its knees. If we do not act now it will be destroyed. We will be in the magician's power to the end of our lives – to the end of our children's lives! He cannot fight us all. We must resist him, whatever the cost; imprison him, drive him from our beautiful city, throw off the chains of fear. Those who have no stomach for a fight, return to your homes. The rest, go through the streets, call up your neighbours, rouse the city. Tell them to take up arms. Bring them to the market square. We will rid the city of this poison; drive Zohak Ali from our gates; send him back into the desert from where he came. Go now. I will wait here.'

The crowd cheered. Among them were several known to be the magician's spies. Fear had protected them. Now they were seized and given a beating. Buoyed up with hope and shouting defiance, the crowd ran off to call the city to arms.

The square emptied. Only Prince Sohrab and a few crippled beggars remained. A score of starving dogs hunted for scraps around the cart wheels. Lost donkeys stood miserably in the sun. Where, Sohrab wondered, were Anahita and Farraj?

High overhead Rosh circled against the blue. He had returned from the mountains where the Bangalore diamond nestled among twigs in his nest, high up a remote cliff face. His mate arranged it carefully among the pebbles, bones and other treasures he had brought her. The black turban had torn free and floated to earth. In the heart of the wilderness, it straggled across thorn bushes.

Rosh looked down on the scene in the market square. His wild eyes saw the crowd disperse, spotted a tasty cat. It slunk into a doorway. He sailed down and settled on the onion-shaped dome of the mosque.

In Fatima's house, meanwhile, the great magician was incandescent with rage. Insulted, humiliated, man-handled, trapped beneath a table, his book of spells stolen, diamond lost, slaves run off! He threw back the broken table and straightened his robes.

The three he hated most in the world were gone but the old woman remained. He longed for revenge and strode into the adjoining room. There she lay, wretched crone, shivering with fear, the bedspread pulled up so far her feet were uncovered. Her feet – he stared. She was wearing shoes. Black shoes with red bows – in bed!

He took two strides and seized the bed-cover.

'No!' She clung tight.

'Let go!' He heaved.

'Sir! No!'

'Let go!' He bared his teeth and raised a fist.

Fatima screamed and covered her face.

Zohak Ali wrenched the bedspread aside. The old witch was fully dressed. And there, resting on her stomach where she had been hiding it, lay his precious book of spells. 'Aaahhh!' He seized it in triumph, battling as she tried to grab it back, and bore it away from the bed.

'Oh, my darling! My precious! My beautiful,

beautiful . . .' He pressed his lips to the crumpled pages and hugged the book to his breast. 'You evil old hag!' He turned on Fatima. 'You'll pay for this. You *and* your hateful son and daughter.'

What should her punishment be? In some excitement he looked round for a flat surface, saw none and set his book on the floor. 'Now!' On hands and knees he threw over the pages. 'Plague — done that. Melting like ice? Head of a pigeon? Spontaneous combustion? Boils? Ah, whirlwind!' That would take care of the house *and* the old woman. Two birds with one stone. He ran a finger along the spell — every word had to be exact. Standing, he turned to Fatima.

Knees drawn up and a corner of dress in her mouth, she watched from the pillow.

'I'll deal with you first.' His reptilian eyes glittered. 'How would you like to fly?'

She did not respond.

It was a long time, years, since he had called down a whirlwind. He would enjoy it. Holding his book firm, he stepped out into the deserted street and raised his eyes. Not a single cloud disturbed the baking blue of the sky. He threw back his cloak and raised an arm. His thin lips moved. A twisting black thread, fine as a fibre of silk, appeared high overhead. Swiftly it spiralled earthwards, thickening by the second. The magician stood back. With a roar like a landslide, the spinning column of air hit Fatima's house.

Instantly all was chaos. The roof was ripped away.

Furniture and rugs spun around the rooms, smashing everything in their path, and vanished into the air. Fatima's sheets were pulled from the bed and whirled away skywards. Her mattress went, too, and the bed. Fatima herself was flung from wall to wall, felt herself lifting and at the last moment managed to grab hold of the window frame. Upside down, she clung screaming in the torrent of wind.

Zohak Ali laughed and waited for her to be plucked away. He wanted to see her flying above the city, arms and legs flailing; imagined her dropping from a thousand metres on to a bone-splintering hillside.

But Fatima was not plucked away, she hung on tight. The magician picked a scrap of wood from the ground. Standing back from the maelstrom within the house, he poked her with it, struck at her knuckles, tried to prise her fingers loose.

He thought he was alone in the alley and was completely unprepared for the assault by Farraj and Anahita who had been hiding in a doorway opposite. The outraged boy hurled himself at Zohak Ali and flung him to the ground.

'Mother!' he shouted above the noise of the wind. 'Hold on! Hold on!'

At the same instant Anahita grabbed the book of spells and wrenched it from the magician's grasp. In two strides she was at the house and flung it through the window into the spinning wind.

'No!' the magician roared. 'Oh, you devil! You fiend!

My book!' He scrambled to the howling window. 'My book! Come back!'

It was too late. The flapping book was caught in the teeth of the whirlwind. Twice it ripped round the room, hitting shelves, rebounding off the chimney piece, striking Fatima a heavy blow on the shoulder. One second it was there, the next it was a hundred metres in the air, high above the rooftops, spinning out of sight amid the rugs and workbenches and cooking pots.

The whirlwind ceased. Fatima crashed to the floor. Zohak Ali clung to the outside of the house, broken-hearted. He turned. There stood the two who had created such havoc in his life. Forgetful, for the moment, of his magic, he drew the curved dagger from his belt and rushed at them.

Farraj and Anahita fled.

He followed.

They darted through an entrance that led to a twisted maze of yards and lanes and workshops. They had grown up in those streets, knew every turning.

Zohak Ali listened. He heard the patter of their footsteps. Left, he turned, and right, and right again, and left. The footsteps faded. He ran on. He was lost.

Fatima lay bruised, dishevelled and weeping. For a full minute she wondered about the madness that had descended upon her house, then sat up and looked around. Nothing remained: bare walls, floorboards and the cloudless sky above. A thin black wisp, the last of the whirlwind, vanished into the blue.

In it, spinning amid the oranges and roofbeams and cushions, was Zohak Ali's book of spells. The pages fluttered wildly, some tore free. Higher it went, and higher, out over the desert and mountains, mile after mile until at length, the whirlwind fading, it fell to earth on a remote sand dune.

A sand ant came to investigate. It sawed off the corner of a page and carried it back to the nest. It was a treasure, a real find. Others came to investigate. The ant led them to the book. They swarmed over it. Busy jaws cut the pages into tiny fragments. A column of ants bore them in triumph across the dune. Waving and wobbling, they vanished underground.

The ants worked day and night. In three days the book was gone. Nothing remained that people might see but a little hollow in the sand. The wind smoothed it over.

Deep below ground the ants nibbled away, reducing the magic to cosy compost.

The Red-Eyed Serpent

Zohak Ali tucked the dagger back into its sheath.
Where was everyone? The lanes, normally bustling
with activity, were deserted. Occasional figures ran
into houses then emerged and ran on. Something was
happening, something he had not been told about. He
did not like it.

An ancient woman sat in a doorway. 'Where is everybody?' he demanded. 'What's going on?'

She stared back at him, dark-eyed, and said nothing.

'Old fool!' he said and pushed her chair over.

Where had that wretched girl and her brother got
to? He hurried along the empty street and turned a
corner. He turned another corner and found himself
in the market square.

The first citizens were assembling. Zohak Ali had no
eyes for them. For there, by the wall of the Great

Mosque at the far side of the square, stood Anahita and Farraj. With them was Prince Sohrab. Of all people, from the Sahara Desert to the Great Wall of China, they were the three he most wanted to meet. Cloak billowing, he strode between the abandoned carts of fruit, poultry and bales of cotton. His long hair flew. His beard jutted ferociously.

'So, now I have you!'

Sohrab, in his golden turban, stood high on the empty cart. Farraj and Anahita, most hated of all, stood on the ground at either side.

'This time there will be no return,' hissed the magician. 'I shall break you into a hundred pieces. The birds will peck out your eyes. The dogs will eat your flesh.' He gestured to the starving mongrels which crept towards them.

'We hear your threats,' answered Sohrab in a ringing voice. 'Evil magician, we have destroyed your book. If you have magic left you may kill me — but you cannot defeat us all. See, the good people of Samarkand are gathering at your back. It is you, Zohak Ali, who had better beware. If I die, I go to Allah; when you die, you go to burning torment.'

The magician turned. The market square was filling. Men, women and children came running from streets on every side. All were armed.

'Ha!' Though he was wicked, Zohak Ali was no coward. 'You think a few peasants with sticks can frighten me?' He threw back his cloak to free his arms. 'You are ready to die? Then see if your Allah—'

Sohrab jumped from the cart and grabbed a thick bamboo pole from a man who stood nearby. 'You will have to fight me first.'

But before he could reach Zohak Ali, a rotten pomegranate hit the magician on his chest. It burst. A fistful of pebbles rattled against the side of his head. He ducked. A shoe, flung from close range, bounced off his shoulder. At the same time the starving dogs closed in. One leaped and bit his hand. Another sank its teeth into the back of his leg. Snarling and snapping, they were all about him. A woman who had lost her children belaboured him with a milking stool. The owner of the bamboo pole snatched it back from Sohrab and waded into the fray. Others followed suit. The magician was surrounded. A donkey, thin as a skeleton and hee-hawing madly, galloped across the square and reared high, slashing with sharp hooves.

Zohak Ali fell. It is likely the angry crowd would have killed him there and then but the magician had not become great, had not, in his earlier life, survived the Chinese dragon pit and crocodiles of the Nile, without having tricks up his sleeve. Now, as the dogs snarled in his face and sticks thudded on his back, he flung out both arms to make himself longer, gave a strange wriggle and shouted aloud.

What he said no one could later remember, but what followed they would never forget. One second the cloaked magician lay writhing on the ground, the next he was gone and a big hissing serpent lay in his place.

The crowd screamed and drew back in panic.

The serpent coiled and struck at people nearby. Venom dripped from its fangs. It was patterned dark green and gold. With red, unblinking eyes it looked all round. The black forked tongue flickered as it tasted the air.

Anahita, Sohrab and Farraj stood by the cart. The serpent slid towards them. They were unarmed. It raised its swaying head as if deciding which to bite first. Their backs were against the splintered wood. Like lightning it struck. Anahita sprang aside. It struck again and fell short.

They retreated round the cart. The serpent pursued them, scales rustling on the dry earth. The wall of the mosque was at their backs. They were cornered.

It raised its head and hissed again, a wicked sound that dried their mouths and made them prickle with fear. Anahita stared into the red eyes and wide red mouth. She saw the venomous fangs. The serpent prepared to strike.

Rosh, meanwhile, high overhead on the dome of the Great Mosque, saw Anahita, saw the big snake. He leaned forward, watching intently, and launched into the air. No one saw him until, with a rush of wings, he crashed past and snatched the striking serpent in his talons.

The snake was big, bigger than himself, the biggest he had ever tackled. There was a brief struggle. But

Rosh was strong. His powerful wings beat the air and carried the lashing snake from the ground. In seconds he was high above the heads of the crowd.

They looked up. Rosh flew higher still, circling above the market and the dome of the mosque, out over the city and back again. At length, a hovering dot against the blue sky, he opened his talons.

Down fell the pierced and writhing serpent, down and down, whizzing through the air. The crowd scrambled out of the way. WHACK! It thudded to earth in the sun-baked market square.

And lay still.

No one dared approach. Then a brave spirit poked it with a stick. A boy nudged it with his toe.

It did not stir.

Word spread through the crowd: the serpent is dead! Zohak Ali is dead!

Cheers filled the air. Strangers hugged each other and slapped each other on the back. Children were hoisted to parents' shoulders to see the dead magician.

'Why is he a snake?' asked a little boy.

'Because that's what he was,' answered his mother. 'A wicked, poisonous snake.'

A little girl pulled her father's hair: 'Daddy, that dog just turned into a boy.'

'Don't be silly,' said her father.

'But he did,' she insisted. 'Look.'

A boy in ragged clothes rubbed his eyes. He seemed lost and confused.

A woman rushed forward. 'My Abdul!' she screamed and crushed him to her heart. 'Where have you been?'

'I – I don't know,' the boy said. 'I thought I was a dog.'

And all over the city, dogs and tethering-posts and flea-ridden cats and mosquitoes were turning back into people. With the death of Zohak Ali all his spells – those that still could – were reversing.

The crowd grew and grew. Somebody set up a shout: 'To the Blue Palace.'

It was taken up: 'To the palace; to the magician's palace; burn the Blue Palace!'

Five thousand people started up the hill. They took the red-eyed serpent by the tail and dragged it in their midst.

Farraj ran to fetch his mother. He found her sitting in the shell of their house.

'I heard shouting,' she said.

He kissed her on the cheek and described what had happened in the square. When Fatima learned that Anahita was safe and Zohak Ali was dead, she dried her tears. Hand in hand they left the house and ran through the empty streets to join Sohrab and her daughter in the crowd.

By this time they were almost to the Blue Palace. A straggle of men, stiff-jointed and confused, emerged from the gates and wandered down the road towards them. Fatima spotted her husband. 'Kashgar!' She ran ahead, nimble as a girl. 'Kashgar! Oh, my husband! My dearest!' She wrapped him in her embrace. 'Where have you been?'

'I don't know.' He picked off some strands of ivy. 'With the tigers, I think.'

'With the tigers?' she cried. 'What tigers? And what's that all over your head?'

He scratched in his hair. 'It looks like bird droppings.'

'Bird droppings? Oh, Kashgar!'

Anahita and Farraj hugged their father. Farraj wept. The family were together again.

Then Fatima and Kashgar turned back to the city while Anahita, her brother and Prince Sohrab continued to the Blue Palace.

The crowd had stopped before the gates. They stared in astonishment. The magician's palace, one of the miracles of Samarkand, was half in ruins. The work of the builders stood firm but the magical additions had ceased to exist. Walls were falling, arches collapsing. The dizzy tower which Zohak Ali had climbed each day was swaying in the breeze. Onlookers scattered as it toppled towards them. With a crash that shook the earth it demolished half the palace and knocked down the wall of the jungle garden.

Anahita waited for tigers and leopards to leap out among the crowd, for crocodiles to snatch legs in their bone-crushing jaws.

Nothing appeared. The people in front, nervously looking to left and right, filtered through the palace gates. Anahita followed. The garden, shrunk to its natural growth, was unrecognizable. Twenty-metre palms were reduced to saplings. Plinths stood empty. She spotted something orange in the grass. It was a toy tiger, made of wood. She found a painted cheetah. Wooden crocodiles, no longer than the span of her fingers, floated in the green pool.

A friend of Farraj found the magician's flag, the black phoenix rising through a ring of fiery stars, lying on the ground. He claimed it as a trophy and ran across the lawn, flying it overhead and pursued by his shouting companions.

When they discovered there was nothing to be frightened of, children ran ahead into what remained of the palace. It was a spectacular ruin. Anahita, Sohrab and Farraj joined them in the magician's study. There lay the unfinished experiments, the broken pots of dust, the cover of the book of spells. She shivered at the memory of their last visit.

A man struck fire. In no time the study was ablaze. Using Zohak's cloak as a torch, he trailed it through the adjoining rooms. The fire spread. Flames leaped above the remaining roofs of the Blue Palace.

The serpent lay abandoned. Green and gold, it straggled in the rubble. Even dead it looked dangerous. A blacksmith, one of the strongest men in the city, took it by the tail and whirled it round his head. With a heave, he sent it spinning into the heart of the fire.

The crowd cheered but their joy was brief. For

strange things began to happen. The timbers shifted. Deep within the blaze there was a noise like whispering and a little chuckle of laughter. The flames grew agitated. Then slowly, from the white-hot belly of the fire, a column of smoke rose into the air. Children screamed as it assumed the appearance of the dead serpent and swayed towards them with burning eyes. Parents drew them back. It was lucky they did so, for with a *bang* that left everyone deaf for a day and a blast of heat that curled their eyebrows, the smoke split apart and there in the middle was Zohak Ali. Was he made of flame or was he wrapped in flame? Did he seem younger or was it a trick of the light? There was disagreement. But everyone saw him, spinning above the burning palace, his head flung back with laughter. For brief seconds he was there, mocking, then like a corkscrew he whirled up into the air and was gone.

The good people of Samarkand stood staring.

The fire died down. In twos and threes they started drifting back to their homes.

'Will he come back?' said the little girl on her father's shoulders.

'I don't think so,' he said. 'If he does, this time we'll be ready for him.'

'He's not a nice man, Daddy,' she said.

Anahita gazed at the smoking ruins.

'What will become of Zohak Ali's treasure?' Farraj asked. 'The cave of gold?'

'What do you suggest?' Sohrab had no need to think.

'The city must be repaired. We shall regild the domes. Improve the water supply. Build a hospital and schools. Help those in need.'

Rosh sailed high overhead. *Ky-ow!* His wild cry drifted on the afternoon air. *Ky-ow!*

Sohrab turned to Anahita. 'I have loved you for your beauty since you handed me a saddle one hot morning a long time ago,' he said. 'Your courage and your goodness make me love you even more. May I ask your father for your hand in marriage?'

She blushed and lowered her eyes.

A little boy at their feet played with his toy tiger.

Anahita smiled. She had never been so happy.